DEAD BEFORE YOU DIE

A DCI HARRY MCNEIL NOVEL

JOHN CARSON

DI FRANK MILLER SERIES

Crash Point
Silent Marker
Rain Town
Watch Me Bleed
Broken Wheels
Sudden Death
Under the Knife
Trial and Error
Warning Sign
Cut Throat
Blood from a Stone
Time of Death

Frank Miller Crime Series – Books 1-3 – Box set

MAX DOYLE SERIES

SCOTT MARSHALL SERIES

Old Habits

DEAD BEFORE YOU DIE

Created with Vellum

For Lou and Christine Iaconetti

ONE

The weather was perfect for killing.

Snow came down heavily, covering everything, making people lower their faces as the relentless storm battered everybody who dared to step out into the open.

He saw her, standing at the bus stop, just like he knew she would be. He'd overheard her talking and knew she'd be there.

The bus will be late in this weather, one of the other office workers had said. Come to the pub with us.

He would have been the first to die if she'd accepted. His plans were not be messed with, but he knew there could be deviations and he would need contingencies. Killing the smarmy sod with the funny haircut would have been an added bonus.

He pulled into the side of the road, ignoring the

honk of a taxi horn. The cabbie looked at him as he drove by, and the man looked back. Almost willing him to get out and come talk to him.

Almost.

That would have meant his plan being rewritten, so he just stared until the taxi driver went on his way.

He rolled the window down and smiled out at her. 'Christine!' he shouted. There was nobody else in the bus stop or else he would have parked around the corner and walked up, pretending he had been in a shop and had casually bumped into her.

The snow was coming down thick and fast now. He could see she was shivering, gently stamping her feet in boots that looked cheap and nasty. Just like her.

She looked at him and smiled. Recognising him. She waved, unsure whether to walk forward or not. He kept the smile plastered on his face while his mind chewed her out. *You're letting the heat out of my car*.

'You want a lift?' Plan A or Plan B was going to kick in now, depending on her answer.

'Oh, I'm fine. My bus will be along shortly. Thanks anyway.'

It could still go either way, depending on how persuasive he was.

'Don't be daft! Hop in. The buses aren't running to any kind of schedule now anyway.' *Hop in now, or I'll fucking kill you where you stand.* One half of his brain told him to jump out and do her now, but the other half, the sensible half, told him to stick to Plan A, for the time being.

'Are you sure?' she replied, looking at him.

He looked at her blankly for a moment, his mind already setting the launch sequence for Plan B, maybe having to open the box on Plan C, but Plan C was only a rough sketch, one that would have revved up his anger level. He'd never had to use a Plan C so far, and by God, if this whiny bitch made him use one tonight, her chances of ever seeing her next birthday were very slim.

She's not going to see it anyway. Bloody clown, he reminded himself.

He almost burst out laughing but managed to cover it as a smile at the last minute.

'Of course I'm sure! There's nobody else here. Maybe the bus just left and you won't know when the next one will be along. It *is* after rush hour.'

After rush hour. He'd made sure she stayed working late tonight. Tonight was perfect; not only were the buses going onto an evening schedule – read *few and far between* – but the atrocious weather was making it worse.

'Oh, okay then.'

Score 1-0 for the psychopathic killer in the fancy car with the heated seats.

He was still staring with the fixed smile when he realised the door was opening. He put the passenger window back up.

'I really appreciate this,' she said, her hair wet around the edges under the hand-made woollen monstrosity that sat on her head.

'Not a problem at all,' he said as Christine put her seatbelt on. The car had four-wheel drive and sat higher than the other, lowly vehicles around him. Quality. That was what distanced him from the other plebs who were driving little hatchbacks with front wheel drive, or, God forbid, rear-wheel drive. People didn't learn. He laughed when he saw them stuck at the side of the road, sometimes *off* the road. Especially when the car wasn't an off-road vehicle. He'd honk the horn, wind down his window and make a face, sometimes followed by a string of obscenities.

Serves them all right.

'There's a heated seat button there,' he said, pointing to it. She looked around, like he'd just suggested she take over the controls of a crippled airliner. He gritted his teeth, again disguising it with a smile. He reached over and pressed the button.

'Ooh, fancy,' she said, making it sound almost sarcastic, but she smiled.

'Better than a ratty old bus,' he said, pulling away from the stop.

The big car cut through the snow like it didn't exist. A radio station played in the background. 'You can change that, if you like,' he said.

'No, it's fine.' She looked at him. 'This is really nice of you to do this.'

I know. 'Don't mention it. This is a hell of a night to be standing about in.'

'You live out west a bit, don't you?' he said.

'Yes.'

'I'm going that way tonight. I can drop you off.'

She made another *don't be silly* face. 'No, it's alright. If you can drop me off close to the station, I'll be fine.'

He grinned again. 'I don't have much to do tonight. Just one thing I have to check on, and then I can drop you off at a station close by. No funny business though!' he said, laughing. 'Seriously, I'd rather you get home safe.'

He drove further on, leaving the lights of the city behind, but the snow filled in the shadows, making things lighter than what they normally would be. The headlights cut through the blizzard as he followed a smaller car.

'What do you have to check on?' she asked.

'I'm going to look at a property I bought, but it's in a bit of disrepair. I just have to swing by to check and see if the contractor left some stuff I ordered. You know what they're like,' he said in a tone that suggested she really did know what they were like. 'Would you mind if we go there first?'

'Of course not. I'm nice and cosy and I can actually start to feel my feet.'

Thirty minutes later, he was pulling off the road, bumping up an old track. 'The road will be paved last,' he said, smiling. The headlight beams cut through the darkness, bouncing off the trees. If she had looked closer, she would see there had been no other wheels up this track recently.

'It's not much further,' he said.

Then the trees thinned out. On the opposite side of the clearing sat an old mansion. It was rundown with boarded up windows. Pallets of building supplies sat out front, covered in snow. He pulled the car close to one.

'Great! He must have got here early. The tiles are marble. Come and have a look. See how beautiful they are.'

He smiled and hopped out of the car before she could argue.

Her smile slipped a bit. He could see her hesitate as he watched her through the windscreen. He smiled and waved at her. She undid her seatbelt and got out into the falling snow.

'See? In there? What do you think of the colour?'

he said, pointing into the middle of the pallet. The headlights shone on the tarp covering what was underneath.

'I can't see anything,' Christine said, peering closer.

She couldn't see any marble tiles because there weren't any. She didn't see his gloved fist coming towards her face. All she felt was something connecting with her chin and then she slumped sideways onto the snow-covered drive.

She didn't feel him lifting her and putting her into the boot of the large car.

He went to the passenger side, rifled through Christine's bag and took her phone out. Then he got back in behind the wheel. He would switch it off back down on the main road, further away from here, then take the battery out and put the phone in a bin somewhere. He knew where there were no cameras.

Then he would take her to her new home.

He drove carefully back down the road and joined the motorway. The car did it easily. It paid to buy quality. Something Christine wouldn't understand.

At least she'd had a lift in it.

Even if it was her last one.

TWO

Two years later

'I've had an offer,' DS Alex Maxwell said as she walked into the kitchen. She had her comfy sweats on and big, furry slippers that looked like something that should be hanging in the butcher's window.

'I feel this is a loaded statement,' DCI Harry McNeil said, pouring himself another coffee. 'Either Coco the Clown wants you to run away with him to join the circus, or somebody wants to buy your house. Either way is good news for you.'

'Coco knows I already live with a clown. So the latter. But it's too low so I'm knocking it back.'

'At least you're starting to get offers. But if you happen to mention in conversation to somebody about your living arrangements, please add that you've been sleeping in my spare room while your house was getting decorated.'

'Instead of letting them think I'm your bit on the side? Why spoil the fun?'

'I'd never hear the end of it from Simon Gregg.'

'Our colleague is more interested in Eve Bell than what you're up to in your spare time.'

'She's a sergeant and he's still a DC, so he'd better watch his P's and Q's.' He added milk to the mug and Alex grabbed it.

'Thank you, Chief Inspector.' She grinned and walked away.

'That's something I'm not going to miss,' he said, pouring water from the kettle into another mug. He popped two slices of bread into the toaster.

They went into the living room and sat at the little table by the window. Snow was falling heavily, covering everything in a thick blanket.

'I still don't understand why you want to sell up. It's a cracking wee flat you have along the road.'

She shrugged. 'Time to move on.' She stared into the coffee for a few seconds, and Harry could sense something was wrong, but didn't want to push. He'd already tried talking to her but she wasn't opening up, and that was when he'd known something wasn't quite right. He wasn't in a hurry to have her move out and into a new place, but he knew that wasn't going to happen any time soon, as she hadn't found a new place yet.

Alex looked at him. 'I don't want this to become an issue, me staying in your spare room. I mean, I could always move back in with my mum and dad for a little while.'

'Don't be daft. They live in Dalkeith. Imagine the commute. Our office is just around the corner.' He stopped, hearing his own voice as whiny and pleading, begging her not to move out. 'Besides, I don't have anybody else to call me a clown.'

'I have to go and pick up a couple of things tonight. Would you go with me?' She looked at him, almost pleading.

Christ, there *was* something wrong. He wished she would tell him. 'Of course. Then maybe we could pick up some Chinese.'

'That sounds good.'

He heard the toaster clunk and he got up and went into the kitchen. He buttered the toast, hearing Alex switch the TV on. She had moved to the settee with her mug of coffee now on the end table and she was sitting with her legs pulled up.

'You want to talk about it?' he asked her.

'No.' There were tears in her eyes. The simple answer told him all he needed to know.

'You know I'll listen without judgement.'

She looked at him and smiled the smile of somebody who had just been crying. 'I know.'

'I mean, you can run away with Coco if you really want to.'

She gave a small laugh. 'I like the clown I have, thank you very much.'

Harry knew he and Alex had a relationship that nobody would understand. He'd spent four years in Professional Standards, investigating other cops, and had very few friends on the force. Most other officers hated him and when he'd started working with Alex the previous spring, it had been a breath of fresh air. She had accepted him, not only as her new boss, but as a friend. He had met her and the other members of his team when they had been working in the cold case unit, which had been punishment for them all.

Now, they were in their own Major Investigation Team, and Harry had hit it off with Alex as a friend. A good friend, with no added benefits, much to the disbelief of others, he was sure.

She was using his spare bedroom and that was it.

They watched some TV, Harry washing his toast down with the coffee. He'd already showered and dressed, an agreement they'd made when Alex moved in. He would use the bathroom first in the morning.

He got up to put his dishes through in the kitchen

when Alex stood up and came over to put her arms around him in a hug.

'Thank you for being there for me, Harry.'

He was unsure what to say at first. 'We're here for each other. I couldn't ask for a better friend.'

She gave him a peck on the cheek and walked out of the living room without saying another word.

And with that, Harry knew there was going to be trouble in her very near future. And he was going to be right there by her side, fighting her battle with her.

THREE

'Will you two stop fighting?' Hector Mann said as his two young kids raced around the living room. One was crying while the other was laughing.

The crying child was Callum, six years old and the butt of his sister's jokes. Eight-year-old Alice was constantly teasing her brother, and this morning was no exception. She had taken something of Callum's and was squealing with laughter as he chased her around the house.

'Will you two behave?' Andrea Mann said, no conviction in her voice. Hector had realised a long time ago that his wife had lost control of her children. Certainly, imposing discipline wasn't at the top of her life skills.

Then he remembered she wasn't working from

home that day and was actually going to drag herself into her office.

'I have an appointment this morning. I'm meeting some important customers of mine.' She took a drag on the cigarette and blew the smoke into the air.

'Are you trying to kill our children?' Hector said, and this time there was no holding back on the lip curling.

'Oh shut up. It's only one.'

'You gave up, remember? And if I remember correctly, you said it was because you didn't want our little ones around second-hand smoke.'

'Christ, Hec, will you get off my back?'

He was going to retort but held it back. He didn't want to start a full-blown fight in front of the kids. Better to bite his tongue sometimes. But he knew what was coming next.

'Can you take them to school?'

His first reaction was to have a fit, but it hadn't worked the last time, and just left him feeling angry, and then he started driving angry, and it was too cold to go to prison if he got out of the car and lamped somebody. He'd rather come home and put his feet up in front of the TV than spend his time in a cell sleeping on a concrete bed or whatever the hell the beds were made of.

'Right you two, get in the car.'

'Shut up!' Callum shouted at his sister.

'You shut up!' Alice shouted back.

'Give me my fucking bag!' Callum screamed, and that seemed to halt them in their paces. Silence descended for a moment.

'Callum!' Andrea shouted after a moment's hesitation.

The children looked at her, then Andrea looked at their father.

'What?' Hector said. 'He didn't get that from me.'

'He didn't get it from watching Sesame Street either,' Andrea said.

'Get in the car,' Hector said before Callum contradicted him. 'Alice, give him his bag back.'

Alice threw the bag at her brother, and Hector thought his son used the derogatory term he called his wife behind her back, so quickly ushered the little boy into his heavy coat.

'Thanks, you're a love,' Andrea said, coming up to him and giving him a peck on his cheek.

Maybe he'd get some alone time with her tonight if he kept in her good books. And if she wasn't wearing the passion-killer socks in bed again.

'I know I am,' he said, smiling, but she had turned away from him and left the room.

Was she having an affair? A midlife crisis? He'd thought he could smell drink on her breath when he'd come home from the office and she had been working at home. Maybe she was inviting the milkman in to discuss the price of low-fat yoghurt. He'd read about it happening to marriages. Hell, one of the blokes in his office had caught his wife entertaining the troops when he'd gone home early one day. Literally. Two squaddies were in his house putting a smile on the wife's face.

Hector didn't want to worry about it. What could he do if she *was* cheating on him? Put in spy cameras?

'Dad!' Callum shouted from the front door. God, the boy didn't half confuse his outdoor voice with his indoor voice at times. The little bugger had even shouted 'You're not my dad!' when they were at the Gyle Centre one day, and his son had refused to take his hand. Christ, talk about taking a beamer.

'I'm coming!' he shouted back, but not at full volume. This voice was halfway between *You're being annoying* and *I'll give you something to cry about in a minute.*

He put on his own heavy jacket and went out the front door.

The kids were jumping up and down.

'Look, Dad!' Alice said, pointing to the end of the short driveway in front of their garages. His friend didn't understand why he and Andrea kept their cars outside, when they each had a garage. Especially in weather like today, when the snow was coming down hard.

His friend just didn't understand that garages were for keeping all their clutter in. Where else would the bikes, the toys and all the rest of the crap they'd accumulated over the years, go?

The BMW was facing the road. Facing the snowman that was blocking it.

'Aw, fuck sake,' Hector said, and the kids giggled.

'Fuck sake,' Callum repeated in a low voice and Alice laughed harder.

'Get in the bloody car, we're going to be late,' he said, and the two kids climbed into the back, Alice helping her brother into his car booster seat. There was one in each car.

Hector got the brush from the garage and quickly swept the snow off his car then got in behind the wheel of the 7 series. He wondered if the owners of the Kellerstain Stables guesthouse further up, had built the snowman. They lived on a private road, just the two houses and the stables that were now a B&B further up. Why would they do that though?

'Can we play with the snowman when we get home from school?' Alice asked.

'No. I have to get him out of the way or else I can't go to work.'

'Aw please, Dad!'

'We can build our own in the back garden.'

'I like that one!' Callum said, staring out through the windscreen. 'I want to play with that one!'

Hector was pretty sure that the inside voice was to be used in the car as well as the house, but Callum hadn't got the message.

Hector put the car in gear and drove forward, hitting the snowman. Instead of exploding into a thousand pieces, snow flew into the air and it hit the front of the car with a thump.

'Fuck me,' Hector said, putting the car in park and opening the door. He heard the kids giggling again, and hoped that Callum didn't start using the words at school.

Jesus. What in the name of God? Hector stepped forward and saw Alice starting to open the rear door. 'Stay in the car!' This time there was no mistaking the *Or I'll skelp your arse* tone he used.

He looked down at what was left of the snowman. And the eyes of the dead woman staring back at him.

FOUR

'Do you know this could be the worst snowstorm we've had in fifty years?' Harry said.

'No, but if you hum it...'

'Mornings are never going to be the same when you buy a new place.'

'Aw, you say the nicest things.'

'How did you know about the offer?' Harry said.

'The solicitor emailed me just before close of business last night and I didn't see it until this morning.'

'That's good. I'm pleased for you. It means that there's already interest in your place so there's going to be more. It's a great area, the Stockbridge Colonies.'

He said it with a smile, but the truth was, he had enjoyed her living in his place again. She had stayed for a few days some months back, and then she'd moved back home. Then when she'd asked if she could crash at his place again while the decorators came in to do up her place for selling, he had agreed. And she'd stayed on while it was put on the market.

'I remember my dad saying that years ago, the time of year mattered a lot more. Now, people can't wait to get their hands on a property.'

'It's true.'

He looked at his watch. It was gone nine and they hadn't made it into the office before getting the call. The request had come in half an hour ago from a patrol unit and the machine had kicked into high gear after that.

A woman, pronounced life extinct at a scene by the duty doctor had resulted in a shout for detectives.

'You ever feel like working from home?' Alex said, turning the car off the main road, the four-wheel drive cutting through the thick snow with ease.

The traffic going in the opposite direction into town was crawling through the blinding snow. They were on the west side of Edinburgh, going past the entrance to the Scottish National Bank world HQ, heading up Gogar Station Road.

Harry was in the front of Alex's new car, gripping the handle above the window like he was about to leap out of a plane on his first parachute jump.

'If I'm going to be home all day, I want it to be in my beach house in Florida. With plenty of people to wait on me hand and foot. A dream I will never realise if you don't keep this car on the road.'

'It's not my fault the gritters haven't been round here.'

'At least with the car being bright red, we'll be seen from the air when you stick it through a hedge and they come looking for us.'

'Quattro all-wheel drive, Harry. This baby will get us to the crime scene without any drama.' She grinned at him. 'You should have worn your brown trousers again. You're sitting there like a wee lassie going out on her first date, all jumpy and sweating.'

He ignored her jibe. 'Audi, indeed. I thought you were going to get a Honda?'

'I knew you'd be wanting a new CR-V after what happened to your old one and we would clash.'

'It's not outfits we're talking about here, it's cars.'

'I just saw an ad for this Audi and decided the insurance money for my old car would go towards this. I miss Betty the Blue Beemer at times.'

'I'm sure Rory the Radge Audi will make up for it.'

'How long you been sitting on that one?' she asked, turning the corner into a private road called Kellerstain.

'Long enough,' he replied.

A sign pointed to where a B&B called Kellerstain Stables was located.

The road, more like a country lane, was long with a white-covered field on one side and a hedge on the other. They were greeted with a multitude of emergency vehicles gathered like a car meet as they approached.

The wind was driving the snow, making it difficult to see as they stepped out, walking round the front of the car.

A uniform came up to them. 'It's round the corner, sir,' he said. 'I'll show you.'

The snow was almost blinding as Harry walked around the other vehicles, some of them patrol cars with their lights flashing.

The forensic tent had been erected and there were uniforms milling about, along with white-suited forensics crew who almost disappeared in the storm.

'Bet you wish you hadn't put your high heels on now, eh?' Harry said.

Alex looked down at her Doc Martens. 'I was going to say the same thing to you.'

The tent was at the end of a short driveway in front of a large, detached house.

Harry and Alex went inside out of the driving wind. Inside, Kate Murphy, one of the city pathologists was crouched down at a macabre figure. She stood up when the detectives entered.

'It's a little hard to tell, but it's a woman. Her

features are almost frozen and there's damage to her. She was hit by a car. She was covered in snow apparently, and the driver thought he was hitting a snowman.'

'Any ID on her?' Harry said.

'There was a wallet in a pocket. One of the forensics team took it. She's not from around here.'

'I don't suppose it's going to be easy to get a time of death?' Alex said.

'Not right now. The weather has played havoc with her.'

'Thanks, Kate.'

They left the tent and went back into the blizzard, Harry tugging his collar up even further. 'Compared to this, that tent was a sauna.'

'I'm putting in for a transfer to The Bahamas.'

Harry shook his head. 'One word: hurricanes.'

'Blow my dreams out of the water, why don't you? If you'll pardon the pun.'

'Let's go and talk to whoever hit that woman. First though... I want to know her name. Let's see if we can find the tech who got her ID.'

The tech in question was a young woman, who Harry would have sworn was one of the kids from the house were she not in a protective suit.

'You have the victim's ID?' he said.

'Yes. It's in the van.' They walked over and she

retrieved the item: a small wallet. The driving licence gave the name of Mhari Baxter.

Harry thanked her after taking a photo of the licence and then they went inside the house to the sound of children yelling and running around.

'Callum!' a woman's voice shouted.

'I told you we should have sent them to school,' a man's voice said.

'They closed the schools, remember?'

'So? Anyway, shouldn't you have checked before you asked me to take them?'

'Oh for God's sake, if you're not going to say anything productive...' The woman talking halted when she came into the hallway from what Harry surmised was the living room.

'And you are?' she said, brushing a loose hair from her face. She was dressed as if she had been getting ready to go to work before somebody had hit the snowman.

'DCI Harry McNeil. DS Alex Maxwell.' They showed their warrant cards.

'You'll be here about the snowman.'

'We'd like a word with... your husband, is it?'

'Yes. He's the one who found her. Go through.'

'We'll need to talk to you as well,' Alex said.

'Fine. I need to put some laundry on.' She walked away and Harry shared a look with Alex.

'Her husband *found* the victim?' he said. 'Found her with the front of his car.'

In the living room, there was a young boy jumping up and down on the settee, a big, leather affair, which had once been pristine, Harry was sure, but which was now doing double duty as an indoor trampoline.

'Callum, get off there. You'll fall and hurt yourself,' the man said.

'No, I won't.'

The man looked at the two detectives who seemed to be enjoying the show. Were it a stage play, it would be called *The Power Play;* about a father and son.

'Callum, that's enough!' the man said.

The boy ignored him.

'Can you tell him?' Mann said.

'We're police officers,' Harry said, 'and if you don't stop jumping on the settee we'll...' He looked at Alex, needing help. *We'll what? Skelp his arse? Put him in cuffs?* Both options, as appealing as they were, might not go down too well with the boss. Harry didn't think the father would bother too much.

The boy stopped all on his own and then jumped down after looking at them. He ran across to a young girl who looked a little older. Harry was sure the little boy had cursed under his breath as the girl laughed at him. They sat at a table and brought crayons out, and Harry was surprised to see colouring books as well, expecting they would have just used the wallpaper.

'Mr Mann?' he said. 'You made the treble nine call?'

'Yes. I couldn't believe what happened.'

'Well, why don't we sit down and you can tell me all about it?' He eyed up a chair, not wanting to sit down on the leather sofa where a pair of small boots had left patches of melted snow.

'Please, find a seat.'

Harry and Alex each moved to a chair. Hector Mann sat down on the settee away from the muddy puddle. 'Kids, eh?' he said, smiling sheepishly, like having your children destroy the furniture was a secret only parents shared.

'What time did you discover the body?' Alex said.

'Oh God, it was a little after eight. My wife wanted me to take the kids today, as she has to go into work. *Had* to go into work. So I was going to drop the little bloody monsters at school.'

Both kids looked round at him. 'Bloody monsters,' the boy said and then giggled as they turned away again.

'That's before we found out they were closed.'

'Then what happened?' Harry said.

'We saw the snowman at the end of the drive. Well, the kids saw it first. They wanted to play with it after school, but I needed to get my car out, and since my wife's is next to mine, I couldn't drive round so I had no other choice but to run it down.' Mann looked down at the carpet for a moment before looking back up. 'God, it was horrible. When I got out of the car, she was lying there, looking right at me.'

'Like she was accusing you,' Andrea said, coming back into the room. There was no sign of any compassion.

Hector Mann ignored her and gave a smirk as his wife sat down on the small puddle.

'Do you know the woman?' Alex asked, getting irritated.

'She was frozen, and her hair was covered in snow, so no, she didn't look familiar.'

'Have you been getting bothered by anybody lately?' Harry said.

'No. My work's going fine. I enjoy being there.'

'What is it you do?'

'I'm an architect.'

'Can I ask what you're working on?'

'The new St James Centre. It's keeping us busy.' Mann stared off into space for a moment. 'I can't help but see that woman's eyes staring back at me. Christ, I'll be having nightmares.'

'Christ,' Callum said and his sister giggled, like she'd put him up to it.

Andrea glanced over, silencing them with a look.

'How many houses are on this private road?' Alex asked.

'Only three of us. The house further down is rented to a professor but he's away just now. Only his housekeeper is there, I believe. The main property is Kellerstain Stables bed and breakfast at the very end of the road. Catriona Corbett owns it, with her husband, Ed. They stay in a house behind the old stables. Which were converted to top-notch suites.'

'Anybody staying there just now?' Harry asked.

'Yes. They're fully booked.' Mann looked at his wife before carrying on. 'I was talking to Ed the other day. He told me.'

Harry wondered if talking to Catriona instead would have been a problem. The look Mann's wife gave him suggested it might be.

He stood, followed by Alex. 'If you remember any other details, please give me a call.' He handed Mann a business card.

Andrea also stood up and showed them back to the front door. 'We called you lot a few weeks ago. We had somebody creeping about outside, but nobody was interested. Look up the incident report that the plod said he was going to submit. You'll see the details.'

Harry looked at Alex, who took a note.

'We'll look into it.'

'Maybe somebody was watching us, Inspector, somebody watching my husband, and then this.'

'And you've no idea who.'

'Not at this moment.'

'Don't hesitate to call if something comes to you. I'll have one of my officers sit with you and your husband for a written statement.'

She closed the door and Harry felt like he had stepped into another world.

'They seem like a match made in heaven,' Alex said. 'And why didn't he mention the peeping Tom when you asked him?'

'God knows. But did you hear that kid? I'm sure he told his old man to eff off.'

'I heard. They don't seem to have a grip of parental skills.'

'Jumping up and down on the bloody settee. If my son had done that...'

'Chance was brought up better than that. I can't imagine him even thinking about it.'

'God knows what his mother has let him get away with now though.' Harry and his wife were divorced and his son now lived with her in Fife.

'He's coming up for sixteen. I'm sure he has a good head on his shoulders,' Alex said.

'He takes after his dad, right enough.'

She smiled at him. 'Come on now, let's not label

the poor lad.'

'You're too funny.'

'We should go and talk to the owner of the guest-house,' Alex said as they skirted round the forensics tent.

'Are we going in Chitty Chitty Bang Bang?'

'Oh, I can't wait to see what car you pick out. I bet you'll have beaded car seat covers in it.'

'You say that like it's a bad thing.'

FIVE

Alex drove carefully, heading further along the private road to the B&B. Too many people came a cropper in the bad weather, thinking that all-wheel drive meant they were driving with a Superman cape on, and nothing would happen to them in the snow.

The guesthouse was further up the road, but the near whiteout conditions made it look like they were driving on another planet.

'Kellerstain Stables,' Harry said. 'When I read the sign, I wasn't expecting to see anything quite so luxurious.'

The wipers batted the snow out of the way, and before them were the guest suites. A sign pointed to the main house, so Alex took that and the little car cut through the deep snow with ease.

Before they had even parked, somebody was

opening the front door to the big house. A tall man, pulling a hood up but making no effort to walk through the snow.

'DCI Harry McNeil, DS Alex Maxwell,' Harry said as they approached.

'I was expecting you,' the man said. 'Edwin Corbett. Come inside. Call me Ed.'

They walked into a wide hallway, and the noise level was positively monastery-like compared to what they'd just left. They dusted the snow off their heads and stamped their boots on the thick doormat.

'I had a visit from a uniformed officer a little while ago. This is absolutely terrible,' Ed said, taking his jacket off.

Harry and Alex were shown into a living room.

'Can I ask you what you know about the incident down at the house?' Harry said as a woman entered the room.

'This is my wife, Catriona. Cat for short.'

'What an ordeal,' she said, ushering the detectives to a seat.

'I was told that a woman had been knocked down by Hector,' Ed said, managing to both look grim and convey to his wife that she should get the kettle on with one look. Cat scuttled away.

'We're not releasing any details until we figure out exactly what happened,' Alex said, shooting down any ideas that Ed was going to be privy to some gossip.

'I didn't know this place existed,' Harry said.

'We bought it a few years ago and converted the old stables to a guesthouse. There are four suites. We also provide breakfast in the sunroom.'

'I was told you're fully booked right now.'

'That's correct, Inspector. We are.'

'Really? I didn't think this was prime visitor season,' Harry said.

'It's not, normally. But we have a group of people here who are in Edinburgh for a conference.'

'Do you have a list of their names?'

'I can write them down. Please, have a seat.' Corbett scuttled away, presumably to fetch a pad and pen.

'Nice place,' Harry said. 'I wouldn't mind living out in the country.'

'Until you had to drive for a Chinese or a fish supper.'

'The peace and quiet would make up for that. This is a beautiful place. Maybe you should consider buying a place in the country and I could crash at the weekend.'

'You know I'm a detective sergeant, right? Where would I get the money to buy a place in the country?'

'I'm not talking about Downton Abbey.'

'I'm a city lassie, Harry. It's not going to happen.'

Corbett came in with a pad. He had written some names on it and handed it to Harry.

He read them out, 'Charlie Henderson, Amber Dodds, Rose Ashland, Lane Mott and Mhari Baxter.' He looked briefly at Alex.

'Lane and Rose are sharing a room. They're good friends,' he quickly added, as if it was 1950.

'Have you seen them all today?' Alex asked.

'No. They skipped breakfast because they had to set up for an early meeting, or something.'

Cat came in with a tray, carrying four mugs and all the accoutrements that go with coffee. She set it down on the coffee table.

Harry thanked her but didn't take a mug. 'Can you tell me about Mhari Baxter?' he asked, ripping the piece of paper from the pad and putting it in his pocket.

'She's nice. They're all nice. All of them are investing in some property or something. Some hotel. They're property investors, something like that. I didn't pay much attention to them when they were having breakfast yesterday.'

Cat gave him a look that said he might have been giving them *too* much attention, but didn't voice it.

'Mhari's nice,' he carried on, 'just like the rest of them. Why are you asking about her in particular?'

Harry was silent for a moment. 'We think it was Mhari who was found dead this morning. There was identification on her, but it's subject to confirmation.'

'Jesus,' Corbett said, and this time, there was no little boy to parrot him. 'Are you sure?'

'It's not definite yet,' Alex said. 'The victim was frozen, so we'll know better after she's been cleaned up at the mortuary. Do you have emergency contact details for the group?'

Cat got up again and disappeared through another door, returning with another list. 'Do the others know?' she asked.

'Not that I'm aware of,' Harry said, looking at Mhari's details. He noted that she was unmarried, yet the driving license indicated she was thirty-two.'

'Did you see anybody suspicious hanging about here recently?' Alex asked.

Corbett shook his head. 'Not that I recall,' he said.

'Mrs Mann down the road said there had been somebody suspicious hanging about and she reported it to the police but nothing came of it.'

'She did tell me,' Cat said, contradicting him.

'Oh well, she told you. But she didn't tell me and neither did you.'

'I think I did. You just don't listen.'

'What did she tell you?' Alex asked, wishing the couple would stop arguing.

'She asked me if I had any male guests in, somebody who would be wandering about, and at the time, I didn't. So she described him to me and said she was going to call the police.'

'What was the description?' Harry asked.

'Middle-aged man, average height, average build. It was dark and he had a hood on, wearing dark clothing.'

'Not much to go on.'

'She saw him more than once,' Cat said, a defensive tone in her voice now.

'Did anybody else see this man?' Alex asked.

'Not that we know of.'

Harry took one of the mugs of coffee, hoping that Cat hadn't laced it with anything. 'Did Mhari mention anything – or anybody – that she was concerned about while she was staying here?' he said, then took a sip of the hot liquid. It tasted quite good.

'Nothing. We hadn't seen her for a few days. She and her friends are booked in until next week. They have a lot of plans to go through. I didn't go into the nitty-gritty.'

Harry asked some more questions, feeling the heat of the room becoming oppressive as his heavy overcoat wasn't designed for wearing indoors.

He put the coffee mug down and stood up followed by Alex who hadn't touched hers.

'Here's my business card. If you can think of anything else, please let us know.'

'I'll be sure to call,' Ed said, taking the card from him.

Outside, the snow was coming down with a vengeance.

They had to wipe the accumulated snow off the windscreen, or rather Harry did, while Alex fiddled with the heated seats.

'I got the pointy end of the stick there,' Harry said, wiping snow off his head as he got in.

'You told me you were a gentleman and who am I to get in the way of chivalry?'

'When are you going to tell Mann about our victim's identity?' Alex asked him.

'Not until we get a formal ID on her. I'm going to have control contact Glasgow Division to have them do the death knock. Mhari Baxter comes from through there.'

He made the call as the wipers swatted the snow away and they headed down to the third house in Kellerstain.

It was a large, detached house, not quite as modern as Mann's, but still quality. There were no tyre marks outside and Harry wasn't sure anybody was in, but they had to check.

Alex parked in the car park at the side of the house

and they rang the bell and waited. The housekeeper answered after the second ring.

'We're police officers,' Harry explained, and they showed their warrants.

'Julia Gregory. Please, come in. What's happening?' She closed the door behind them. 'I saw all the police vehicles going up. Is everything okay?'

She could have been anything between fifty and sixty-five, depending on whether her hair colour was natural or out of a bottle.

'Unfortunately, there's been a suspicious death outside Mr Mann's house.'

She clapped a hand to her mouth for a moment. 'Oh God, that's terrible. Please, come through to the kitchen.' She stopped short of adding *and tell me more* but the implication was there.

She put the kettle on in the huge kitchen. An Aga stove stood in pride of place, and the house was immaculate, as it should be when you hired a housekeeper.

'Did something happen to Andrea?' Julia asked, her eyes flitting between the two detectives.

'No. It doesn't involve any of the Mann family members. There was a victim covered in snow.'

'Oh dear, that's terrible.'

'Mrs Mann said she reported seeing somebody acting suspiciously near here recently. Did you see anything?' Alex said.

'Oh no, dear, I haven't seen anything. Nothing like that. Is she sure?'

'It's what she reported. But did you hear or see anything out of the ordinary last night?'

'No. I lock up early and I have a wee place tacked onto the back that's my own living quarters. I still take my job seriously when the professor's away. He and his wife have been very good to me, but I don't know what I'll do when they retire.'

Harry sensed there wasn't much else they could get out of the woman, so he stood up.

'Keep your doors locked at all times, Mrs Gregory. Just in case.'

'Oh my. Yes, I will. I do wish the professor would allow me to have a dog. It doesn't have to be a big one, just something that barks a lot.'

'Meantime, please be alert,' Alex said. 'And don't hesitate to call treble nine if you see or hear anything suspicious.'

'I won't.'

They left and got back in the car.

'I think she'll be safe,' Harry said. 'Mhari Baxter wasn't chosen at random.'

'Makes me wonder if she was the first or if there are others.'

SIX

'Paul!' Hector Mann said, getting out of the car. The big BMW's xDrive all-wheel drive system had brought them safely down the old driveway from the hotel's back entrance.

The others followed Mann's lead and walked over to the young man who was standing inside the overhang at the entrance to the old hotel.

Paul Fox smiled and shook Mann's hand, then the others as he was introduced. 'Charlie Henderson, Amber Dodds, Rose Ashland and Lane Mott. Your prospective buyers.'

'Good to meet you all. Please, come away inside. I unlocked the door already so please go in and we'll have a wander around and answer any questions you may have.'

Inside, the reception area was eerily quiet. They

stood looking at the old wood panelling, and the beautiful staircase opposite the reception window that led up to the upper floor.

'How many bedrooms again?' Lane Mott asked. Her expression looked like she had just stood in something.

'Twenty-five in the extension out the back, fifteen suites in this main building. There are five function suites, including the main ballroom which was used for—'

'I didn't really ask that, did I?'

'No, you did not.' He smiled.

Charlie Henderson started snapping off photos. 'There's going to be a cost analysis,' he said to Fox.

'Of course. Take as many photos as you like.'

'How long has it been empty?' Rose asked.

'Two and a half years.'

'Why so long?' Amber said, following the others down a hallway. Fox switched the lights on.

'There was another buyer, a man who lived in London, but he died before the purchase could be completed. There was somebody else interested, but I wasn't involved with it back then. I'm not sure why that fell through. The boss was dealing with it then.'

'Are there many people interested in it just now?' Henderson again, snapping photos like a Japanese tourist.

'No, there's nobody else at the moment, but we expect that to change in the spring. Which is not far away. Your group is the first to learn of the price reduction and we're sure that will attract more customers. As you may have noticed, landscaping work was begun before the snow came, to make it more attractive. This will be completed, even if you buy the building. It's part of the deal.'

'It's in remarkable condition,' Hector Mann observed.

'It's been well maintained. The heating has been kept running, and the electricity. The owner didn't want to lose a fortune just because some pipes froze and ruptured,' Fox said.

'That makes sense,' Rose said. She smiled at Fox, who smiled back at her.

They reached the ballroom. 'This was a very popular wedding venue. Here, tables would be set up and the stage at the end would have the band playing.'

'Really? A band playing on the stage? How novel.' Lane's tone was sarcastic.

Fox's face turned a little bit red. 'Yes, well, as I said, there are another four conference rooms, different sizes. Oh, and there's the bridal suite upstairs. Some newly married couples would stay up there. In fact, they had what was known as a *wedding run*. The couple would get into the hotel's minibus, as if they were being driven to the airport, and it would go down to the main road and cut through Ratho Station and come back up into the hotel by the back way. The couple would then sneak up the back stairs with a night porter who would let them in...'

Lane held up a hand. 'I'm sure somebody might find that interesting, but I don't see how that drivel can help us decide.'

'I'm sorry, I just read every detail of the hotel in the paperwork that was prepared.'

'Just stick to the facts, sonny. We don't need any embellishment.'

Mann turned to her and gave her a look.

'Of course. Some of my other clients want to know about every nut and bolt, so I try and provide all the details.'

Lane had dismissed him and walked away.

'What the hell are you doing? Talking to him like that?' Mann said in an angry whisper to her. 'He's a friend of mine, and if anybody can help us get in here, he can.'

'Get over yourself,' Lane said.

'Just don't fuck this up, Lane. I mean it.' He glared at her for a second before walking away.

SEVEN

By mid-afternoon, the temperatures had fallen and the air felt brittle against skin.

Harry was in the incident room with the rest of his team. The room had been set up and the kettle came to a boil shortly before two figures walked into the room.

'That's my favourite sound, the kettle clicking off,' DCI Jimmy Dunbar said, smiling at Harry.

'Even better, since we're visitors, we don't have to inflate the kitty,' DC Robbie Evans said, grinning.

'Listen to you. Get some money in there, and for your lip, you can put mine in as well,' Dunbar said.

'Good to see you again, Jimmy,' Harry said as they shook hands. 'How's life treating you?'

'Each day is a step closer to retirement, my old son. Counting the days.'

'Really? How long you got?'

'Oh, about two thousand days. That's over five years, in case you need to take your socks off to count,' he said to Evans' back.

Harry made the introductions. 'You already know Alex. This is DS Eve Bell, plus we'll have however many bodies we deem fit to help us. Two of my team are down at the mortuary. The pathologists are doing the PM just now. But I have to admit, I was surprised when they said you were coming through.'

Dunbar sat at a desk. 'They originally wanted us to bring the family member through for the ID but the weather isn't fit for it. Besides,' he waved a manila folder at Harry, 'they want us to show you this.'

'What is it?' Alex asked.

'A cold case. From two years ago. A young lassie found dead just like your victim this morning. Covered in snow. Been dead for a week. She had been frozen, as in stuck in a freezer, before he brought her out and covered her in snow.'

'Do you think that could have happened to our victim?' Eve asked.

'I'm on tenterhooks waiting to see what your pathologist has to say,' Dunbar said. 'The dental records were emailed over and we're waiting for that result too.'

Evans made the coffees and dished them out.

'I already got them,' Harry said. 'Her identity was

confirmed. Mhari Baxter, just like the driving licence said.'

'I didn't think there would be any doubt.'

'Are you going back tonight?' Harry asked, looking at the clock.

'No, we're here for the duration. We got rooms at the wee hotel along the road. The Raeburn.'

'Just round the corner from me. They must be serious to have you stay over.'

'It has all the hallmarks, Harry. Here, let me put this stuff up on a whiteboard.' He looked over at Evans. 'Robbie, get this stuff up on the whiteboard.'

Evans made a face but took the envelope anyway. 'Yes, Mr Dunbar, sir.'

'Shut up and get the stuff up.'

'I'll help you,' Eve said.

'Thanks, ma'am.'

'You can see I've just about got the boy whipped into shape,' Dunbar said. 'Now all I need is a cattle prod to give him a good buzz in the knackers and we'll be laughing. I'm sure the laddie was dropped on his heid.'

'My mother said she never dropped me,' Evans retorted without turning round.

'I meant last week when you were out gallivanting.'

'Just 'cause he's in his jammies by eight o'clock,' Evans said to Eve.

'I heard that. Just remember who has to authorise your expenses. It'll be a cup of hot chocolate for you in the hotel tonight.'

'Aye, right. This is Friday. I say we should hit the town.' Evans grinned at Eve. 'What about it? Show us around?'

Before Gregg could answer, Dunbar threw a pen at him. 'Just hurry up and get those photos up on the board.'

'How was the M8?' Harry asked. That was the main motorway link between Glasgow and Edinburgh.

'We took a patrol Land Rover. Bloody big tank it is. But Robbie was driving like an old woman going to church.'

'I got us here, didn't I?' Evans said, still not looking at his boss.

'Aye, but we left three weeks ago.'

'It didn't stop him having a nap.'

'For your information, I closed my eyes so I could run the case through my head without distractions.'

When they were standing looking at the whiteboard, Dunbar started telling them about the previous victim.

'Christine Farr, aged thirty-five. Lived alone in a small flat. She was a bit of a loner. No real friends to talk of, no boyfriend or husband. Divorcee.' Dunbar stood and tapped at one of the photos that had been stuck to the whiteboard with a magnet.

'She was finally reported missing ten days after she was last seen,' he said, carrying on. 'She left her office building in a snowstorm, and was never seen alive again. Her boss reported her missing, calling us and telling us he hadn't spoken to her in over a week and he was worried about her. There was no answer at her flat. They tanned the door in but found nothing. The following day, some kids playing on sledges in a park reported seeing an arm sticking out of a snowman and when the uniforms inspected it, there she was. Covered in snow.'

'Were there any signs of cause of death when you first arrived?' Alex asked.

Dunbar looked at her. 'Nothing. There were no visible marks on her when she was found, and nothing obvious at her post-mortem. It was only after they cut her open that they discovered she'd been frozen alive.'

'Was she left out in the field all that time?' Eve asked.

Dunbar looked at him. 'No. The kids had been playing in the park every day since it had started snowing, and that was the first day they'd seen it, so Christine had to have been put there overnight. We checked local CCTV but nothing jumped out. There weren't many cameras in the vicinity though.'

'Any DNA results?' Alex asked.

'No. Nothing. She was clean. Literally.'

'Any suspects?' Harry asked.

'Nobody. She worked in an office, and we interviewed everybody she worked with, including the cleaners, but nothing. She had a half day, and left her job. We went through her private life, but she didn't have anybody wanting to harm her, that we could find. She had an ex-boyfriend a couple of years before she died, but he was already married and had moved up north. He had an alibi, which held up. Her ex-husband too, had moved on and had a cast-iron alibi.'

Dunbar tapped another photo of the young woman. 'For all intents and purposes, she was abducted by a stranger and held somewhere. He killed her before dumping her.'

'Any more like her?' Harry asked him.

'Nothing. It would appear that Christine was his first and only victim, which would suggest a more personal case, but nothing came of it.'

'Until now,' Alex said.

'We need to look for any connections between your victim then and ours now.'

Just then, the door to the incident room opened and two members of Harry's team walked in.

'DCI Dunbar, this is DI Karen Shiels, DC Simon Gregg,' Harry said, making the introductions.

Dunbar pointed to Evans. 'My sergeant, Robbie Evans.'

'What's the news?' Harry asked as the kettle was brought into service again.

'Mhari Baxter was indeed dead before she was covered in snow. The tissue had damage, indicating she was deep frozen, like she was in a freezer before she was put on display,' Karen said.

'The owner of the guesthouse, Ed Corbett, told me Mhari hadn't been seen for a couple of days. Maybe she was abducted and taken somewhere and killed,' Harry said.

'Considering that place is out of the way, I'd be willing to bet that Hector Mann was targeted for some reason,' Alex said. 'Somebody left Mhari in his driveway to give him a message.'

'I'd like to speak to him,' Dunbar said.

'We can go there again and have another chat,' Harry said. 'We'll need to get your division to talk with Mhari's family, see if any of them know of Mann. Get some background on her. The usual stuff.'

Dunbar nodded. 'I'll make a call.'

'We can go up speak to Mann tomorrow. That'll give the crime scene people time to get a lot more processing done.'

'Agreed. It will give my team back in Glasgow time as well. They can see if there's any connection between

Christine from two years ago and this lassie. Meantime, we'll regroup here tomorrow. Even though it's Saturday. There's overtime in it,' Dunbar said. He looked at Harry. 'We've already been authorised, so I'm assuming likewise from the east coast side?'

'It is. I've already spoken to Jeni Bridge, our commander, and we're covered.'

'Does that mean a pint is covered tonight as well?' Evans asked.

'It means you're putting your hand in your pocket.' He shook his head and leaned in closer to Harry. 'They wanted us to share a room as well, to cut down on the costs. I told them there's more chance of me poking my right eye out with a fork than sharing a room with heid the baw. So they relented.'

'That's fine,' Evans said. 'When I pull a lassie at the dancing, I won't have to tell her to ignore grandpa in the next bed.'

'Shut up. You're here to work. Bloody pull. What way is that to talk about women?'

Evans grinned and looked at the female officers, who weren't amused. 'You know what I mean. When I ask a very fine Edinburgh lass back to my room for a game of darts or something.'

'How about showing us your local, DCI McNeil?' Dunbar said.

'Sounds good. We have a couple, but the St

Bernard's is a good wee place. I've only seen one fight in there a long time ago.'

'Nobody gets rolled in the toilets then?'

'Not when I'm in there.'

'How about eight?'

Harry looked at Alex, remembering he was supposed to be helping her at her flat. She nodded.

'Eight's fine.'

'Great. We'll get a scran at the hotel and see you in the pub afterwards.'

EIGHT

Alex was pacing about Harry's living room, chewing at a fingernail, stopping to look out the window before carrying on.

'What's wrong?' Harry asked.

'What? Oh, nothing. I'm just waiting for you to get ready.'

They had changed plans, since Jimmy Dunbar had come through from Glasgow and had ordered Chinese *before* going to her flat.

'Well, I'm ready now. We taking your car?'

'Not if we're meeting Jimmy in the pub.'

'DCI Dunbar.'

'Oh, here we go with that, *Don't call senior officers by their first name* lecture. If we're having a drink, then it'll be fine.' She headed out of the living room and

Harry decided to grab a beanie hat, not something he usually wore.

'Wow. Covering up your noggin. If I didn't know any better, I'd think that was a disguise so Vanessa didn't see you sneaking out with me.'

'I don't care what she sees, remember? I left her behind last year and this is the new me. Besides, we're colleagues, one of whom rents a room from the other.'

'That's it, spoil the illusion that we're fooling around behind her back.'

'There's a reason they're called the *ex*, you know,' he said, locking the front door. And with that, her mood changed. He could sense it more than see it, but she made a brave attempt at small talk as she gripped his arm.

They walked along Raeburn Place, the Friday night festivities beginning to take shape, as younger versions of themselves went on a night out, scantily clad youngsters attempting bravado despite the weather.

The snow had stopped now, leaving behind its trail of destruction on the pavement.

'I'm anxious to hear if Christine Farr has any connection to Mhari Baxter,' he said as they crossed the road further down.

'Me too,' she said, spinning round as somebody ran past.

'You okay?' Harry asked, hunching up inside his coat.

'Of course I am, but being coppers, we can't be too careful.'

Harry knew she was spinning him a line but kept quiet.

When they reached St. Bernard's bar, she suddenly stopped, pulling on his arm.

'Maybe I should just go round to my flat myself,' she said.

'Why? What's wrong?'

Alex hesitated for a moment. 'Nothing. It's just cold, that's all.'

Harry looked at his watch. 'We still have an hour before Jimmy and Robbie meet us here.' He looked her in the eyes. 'You want to tell me what's going on, Alex? I'll listen without judgement, I already told you that.'

She let out a breath into the cold evening air. 'Okay, walk with me and I'll tell you.'

They rounded the corner, heading down St Bernard's Row, heading towards Alex's flat on Reid Terrace.

'I wasn't exactly honest with you when I first met you last summer,' she said, not wanting to look at him as they walked, but she still hung on to his arm. 'I told you I had split with my ex five years before. That wasn't true. It had been more like a year.'

Harry looked puzzled. 'Okay. I had only just met you at the time. But what was the difference?'

She shrugged. 'I don't know. I suppose I wanted you to see me as somebody who had her life in control, ex far away in the background, me being a sergeant who was going places, not some loser who was stuck in the cold case unit. I wanted to show a front where I had successfully moved on, just like he had. Not some pathetic loser.'

'I never thought you were a loser.'

'See? That's because I gave you a different impression.'

'And he's back on the scene now, isn't he? He's going to be here tonight. That's why you want me to come along with you.'

'Yes. Sorry. I can understand you being angry at me.'

'I'm not angry, but I wish you had told me about it sooner. You want me to pretend I'm your boyfriend, don't you?'

'Not if he asks you outright.'

'Just to give the impression.'

'Yes. But it's a lot to ask.'

'It's fine.'

They walked over the small bridge that spanned the Water of Leith. 'So why sell the house now?'

'He didn't just move on. I heard he met somebody

else, not the woman he cheated with, but another woman, and they have a baby now. He asked me about selling it and giving him what he's due. Which is fair enough I suppose. I told him he needs to pick his stuff up. I told him an offer had been made and I was accepting it.'

'But you haven't accepted it, have you? That's what you said this morning.'

She let out a deep breath, where it plumed in the cold air. 'I thought about it, and then I called the solicitor this afternoon and told him to take the offer. It's not what I wanted but it will give Ian his money and I can start fresh.'

The street didn't look as dark with the snow filling in the shadows, but the river running along to the left was a dark ribbon cutting through the night. There was nobody standing waiting, up ahead. But Ian would be foolish to be standing outside, Harry thought. Maybe the guy was sitting in a car.

Ian Wallace was indeed sitting in a car. He got out when he saw Alex approaching. His face was like thunder. His hands were tucked into his pockets and he made no attempt to bring one out to shake Harry's.

He wasn't overly tall but he was big-built with broad shoulders.

'Ian, this is my boss, DCI McNeil.'

'Whatever. Can we just get on with it?'

'Just like that? You call me up, order me around, telling me that you wanted your half as quickly as possible, and I'm supposed to dance, is that it? Just remember who started all of this.'

'Oh, here we fucking go. Nag, nag, nag. My girlfriend is waiting on me. You know, the one who doesn't moan when I come in pished.'

'Not only me, but your watch commander too, I believe.' Alex's face was starting to crumble so Harry stepped in.

'Maybe it's best if we get this over and done with.'

'Maybe you should watch your mouth, pal.' Wallace took a step towards Harry, who stood his ground and smiled. Wallace had his back to the man who had silently come up behind him.

'You'd be the one who would make me do that, eh?' Another step closer.

'No, but he might.' Harry nodded over Wallace's shoulder.

DS Robbie Evans walked closer to Wallace. 'You got a problem here, pal?'

'Who the fuck are you?'

Evans grinned. 'Somebody who will knock your fucking front teeth out.'

An older man stepped out from behind the stone steps at the next house. 'You better believe him, pal.

Where we come from, we deal with harder school lassies than you.'

'Is that right?' Wallace said. 'I just need to make one phone call and I'll have a dozen of my mates round here who will do more than knock your fucking teeth out.'

Jimmy Dunbar brought his warrant card out. 'And we'll have a dozen of ours round here, only difference is, we'll have you all in handcuffs. And as you know, the cells can be a dangerous place.'

'Just go and get your stuff and say goodbye to Alex,' Evans said.

Wallace turned away from the two men and gave Harry a dirty look. 'Let's make this quick. I have somewhere to go.'

He walked up the steps with Alex, and Harry indicated with his head for Evans to follow, which he did.

'I appreciate you coming round, Jimmy,' Harry said. 'I could have dealt with him on my own, mind, but...'

'But you don't want to fall on the ice and break a hip. I'm with you on that one. Wee Robbie, however, has no such worries and he would have given that big bastard a good tanking. Robbie's an ex-boxer.'

'Well, the beer is on me tonight.'

'You won't get any arguments from us.'

A few minutes later, Alex and Wallace came down

and Wallace put the bags in the back of the hatchback. Evans followed.

'I won't forget this,' Wallace said to Harry. 'This isn't over.'

'Any time you want to go boxing, give me a call,' Evans said.

Wallace sneered at him and got into his car and drove off.

'Thanks for being here,' Alex said. Then she turned to Dunbar and Evans. 'All of you. Harry didn't tell me you were coming.'

'No problem,' Evans said. 'It's been a wee while since I went boxing with anybody.'

'Aye, well, Jim Watt would have been proud of you tonight, but let's see if we can have a quiet beer without you throwing anybody through a window,' Dunbar said, clapping his hand on Evans' shoulder.

They started traipsing up the narrow street and Alex looked at Harry. 'I appreciate you bringing reinforcements, but I could have handled Ian.'

'Sometimes it's nice to have your friends along for the ride.'

Harry looked ahead, picturing in his mind how it all could have gone pear-shaped. Would he have gone boxing with Wallace? Of course. He'd been in many a scrap but he'd seen how Alex had been feeling the past few days, and had known this was going to be no ordinary encounter. She was a tough detective, but even he could see that Wallace had her rattled.

'First night in Edinburgh and we're nearly in a pagger. I'm liking this place already,' Evans said.

'The only time I want to see your hands coming out your pockets is when you're heading up to the bar,' Jimmy Dunbar said. 'Cocky wee sod.'

Evans grinned.

NINE

.

'What you for?' Harry asked when they got to the pub.

'Cheers, Harry, I'll have a lager, and the same for the boy.'

They sat down beside Alex as Harry got the drinks.

'This is a rare wee watering hole here,' Dunbar said. 'What do you think, Robbie?'

'Aye, nice wee boozer for the old 'uns.'

'Hey, this is my local too, and I'm not exactly a granny,' Alex said.

Evans held up a hand. 'No offence meant, Alex.'

'Offence taken.'

He grinned at her. 'Cheers, boss,' he said as Harry came with the first drinks. He went back to get the other two and sat down.

'Did you hear back from your team?' Harry asked. 'Sorry to talk shop, but you know...'

Dunbar held up a hand. 'Say no more, squire. I find it hard to switch off when I go home as well. I end up talking to the dog. More because he listens, doesn't get bored and always laughs at my jokes.'

'Every time I've seen him, he's been out for the count on the carpet,' Evans said. 'I thought you had bored him into unconsciousness.'

'You've been round to my gaff twice, and one of those times was in the middle of the night when I was sleeping.'

'I stayed over one night after a Christmas party. His missus let me sleep in the spare room with the dog.'

Dunbar drank some of his pint. 'Anyway, to answer your question, Harry, I did indeed get a call from one of my DIs. He went through the Christine Farr file for me before he knocked off for the weekend. There wasn't any mention of Mhari Baxter being associated with her. They both come from Glasgow, but no connection that he could see. It was just a quick glance right now, as he's up to his armpits in a case, but he'll get somebody to go through it more closely on Monday.'

'Fair enough. We're going to be interviewing Hector Mann tomorrow.'

'There was one thing in the report though; Christine Farr reported somebody in her office for harassment. Roger Pollock, his name was.'

'Roger Bollocks,' Evan said.

Harry looked at him.

'That's what they called him behind his back.'

'The laddie's right. That's what we were told. Nobody liked him.' Dunbar pulled out some money and handed it to Evans. 'Go and get another round in.'

'Put your money away, Jimmy,' Harry said, handing the young sergeant some cash.

'Come on, Alex, give me a hand with the glasses, will you?' Evans said.

She got up from the table and they went up to the bar. It was usually busier in here on a Friday night, but the weather was keeping people indoors.

'What was the result of the complaint, Jimmy?' Harry asked.

'The guy was fired. He had been following her and making sexual innuendos, that kind of stuff.'

'Was he in the frame for it?'

'He was indeed, and we had him in for a chat, but turns out the sod had a cast-iron alibi. The day Christine left work in a snowstorm in the west end of Glasgow, Pollock was working in Kent. That's where he had moved after he got fired, apparently.'

'I don't need to tell you that if it was some random attack, then we've got nothing,' Harry said.

'Exactly. That's why me and the laddie got sent

through here, Harry. They want to cover all the bases. If we can't find any links, then...'

'It's a coincidence?' Harry said.

'Yeah. But you and I know all about coincidences.'

'As I said, we'll look into it a bit deeper. Maybe this Hector Mann will have remembered something else.'

'Especially since we've confirmed the victim's identity.'

Alex and Evans brought the drinks over.

'I'd like this Pollock guy looked into again.'

'I'm having him pulled in for another interview,' Dunbar said. 'And I have them going over his background again.'

Harry drank some of his pint. 'I wonder why the snowman was left in front of Hector Mann's car and not his wife's?'

'Maybe whoever killed her didn't like BMWs.'

'I think it's a bit more than that, Jimmy.'

'You think he was targeted?' Evans said.

'I do.'

'We just need to figure out where the connection is,' Alex said.

'Hopefully we'll find out tomorrow,' Harry said.

TEN

Vanessa Harper poured herself another glass of wine and looked out of her living room window again. She put the light out and sat on a chair, watching the snow coming down. It was a beautiful sight, covering everything in a soft, white blanket. Peaceful and quiet, just right for drinking herself into unconsciousness.

Well, not that bad, but there was certainly not going to be anything left of this bottle. Or the other one waiting for her.

She could see Harry McNeil's flat from here, and just thinking about him made her ache inside. She mentally kicked herself every day now. She'd had a good thing and she had blown it with him. So what, he wanted to keep his flat on. What was the big deal? But no, that wasn't good enough for her. She had wanted Harry to make more of a commitment, to give up the lease on his flat and move in with her permanently. He had hesitated, and she had taken that as a sign that he didn't want her as much as she wanted him.

And now she was alone. She'd even made a display of herself before Christmas. Taking him to a restaurant, faking a text from work, and then making sure Harry saw her new boyfriend, right after she'd told him all about her new relationship. She wondered if he knew that the *boyfriend* was really a friend of hers, and a gay one at that?

She would never know now.

She looked down towards the bowling club, the hedges just white rectangles. Vanessa couldn't see Harry's stair door, but she could see his windows on the top floor of his building, and she watched, waiting for the living room light to come on. Her house was on a hill which gave her a bit of an advantage, but she wasn't as high as she would have liked.

She supposed he was out with her again. The young woman who worked with him. That should be her, Vanessa, up there with him not Alex Maxwell.

She finished her wine and put the glass down on a side table and picked up her iPhone. Should she call him? Just to hear his voice or to interrupt his plans? A bit of both.

Then she saw him. He was walking round the snow-covered hedge at the end of his road, walking towards her house. Was it Harry? It had to be. He was dressed in black, just like the previous night, when he had walked past her house then had doubled back and had stood looking at her from outside. Of course, he'd had a scarf wrapped round his face from the cold, and had worn a hat, but it was him alright. She could tell. Maybe he looked a bit heavier because of the layers, but it was Harry. Wasn't it?

She felt the hairs go up on the back of her neck. The guy was just standing staring at her. She got up in the dark and closed the curtains without putting any lights on. She put her glass down and went through to the hallway after hearing a noise. Just to check she had locked the front door.

There was something on the floor. An envelope.

She picked it up and opened it.

Inside was the drawing of a hangman. Little lines were drawn underneath, the letters filled in.

They spelled out her name.

It was touching ten o'clock when Jimmy threw back the last of his pint.

'I don't want you to think I'm a lightweight, Harry, but I have to make a call to my DI back at the hotel.'

'Aye, I was going to head along the road. Don't want to go out for the interviews tomorrow blootered.'

Evans looked at his watch. 'What about you, Alex? You heading off somewhere?'

'Nah. I was just going to head off home. Well, you know, Harry's place. I'm staying in his spare room...'

'No need to explain,' Dunbar said.

'No, seriously,' she said but her face was already starting to go red.

'Holy moly, do the boozers shut down at ten on a Friday night?'

'Shut your cakehole, Robbie,' Dunbar said. 'We didn't come through to Edinburgh so we could go and look at the crime scene half-jaked.'

'I hope you packed your Horlicks, sir.'

'Again with the cakehole. I'm going back to the room to work. Then I have to call the missus.' Dunbar finished his pint.

'And Scooby.'

'That dog likes him more than me.'

'That's because I tell him exciting stories. Not tales of when I was on traffic duty.'

'You'll be back on bloody traffic duty when we go home, make no mistake.'

'We'll pick you up at the hotel around ten?' Harry suggested.

'We'll pick you up, Harry. We've got that big

motor. After we have some breakfast. Robbie can drive. Wear your brown trousers.'

'I'll be hitting the hotel gym,' Evans said.

'Unlike the last time when we were in the Highlands and you were hugging the lavvy.'

'It was those iffy tattie scones. God, they were like bricks.'

'Aye, nothing to do with all the Tennent's you had.'

Harry and Alex stood up.

'Catch you tomorrow, lads,' Harry said.

'Goodnight, sir,' Evans said. Then he smiled at Alex. 'Any blowback from earlier with Wallace, give me a call.'

'I'm sure he learned a lesson.'

Outside, the snow was falling again. 'Grab a fast black?' Harry said.

'I think that might be a good idea.'

There were plenty of cabs with their orange For Hire lights on. Raeburn Place was a corridor for taxis heading back up town for more fares.

One cab pulled away from the side of the road and put his light back on but before Harry could put his hand out, the cabbie honked the horn and wound down the passenger window. He waved Harry over.

'As I live and breathe!' the man said. 'Harry McNeil!'

Harry smiled when he recognised the driver. 'Dan! How's things?'

'Hop in and I'll tell you.'

'Great. We were just going home.' He opened the door for Alex and she got in the back. Harry told him the address. 'DS Alex Maxwell, this is Dan McLeod. He's one of us.'

'Was,' McLeod replied.

'You left the force?' Harry said as they sat back.

'I did indeed. I couldn't take any more of their nonsense, Harry. It's all politics now. I got fed up with all of that.'

'There were big changes right enough.'

'I got out while the going was good. Now I'm my own boss. I rent this cab off a guy and I work my own hours. I have it for twelve hours every day and the owner's not bothered how many hours I drive, so long as he gets his rental money at the end of the week.'

'Well, good for you, pal. I'm pleased to see you doing so well. And you haven't put on any weight.' Harry grinned.

'It would be too easy, but I take care of myself.' The roads had been ploughed but were getting covered again. McLeod took it easy until he turned into Comely Bank Avenue, then right into Harry's street. He stopped at the steps after following Harry's instructions.

'How about a beer one night, Dan?' Harry said.

'Jesus, I would love that. All my old muckers are always too busy, or working stupid shifts. I keep in touch with a few of course, but I don't get to see them enough. What about you? You still in Standards?'

'No. I got transferred to MIT about six or seven months ago. I run my own team. I got DCI too with the transfer.'

'Aw, buddy, that's magic. Nobody better deserves it.' McLeod turned to Alex. 'I'm assuming you're on the team?'

'I am, Dan. I was in the cold case unit until Harry took over the MIT. I got transferred.'

'That's great. You won't have a better boss than this man.'

'I know.' She smiled at Harry.

'Listen, I drive this taxi most nights but I have a couple of nights off during the week when it's quiet. Maybe we could get a pint then?'

'That would be great. What night?'

'How about Monday? Or Tuesday? Either one for me. I don't do much on my nights off.'

'Me neither.'

McLeod laughed. 'Rock 'n' roll lifestyle, eh?'

'Give me your number, Dan, and I'll give you mine.'

'How about I go and get the kettle on?' Alex said.

Harry sat back and let her out. 'I won't be long.'

'She's a nice girl,' McLeod said.

'She's just my roommate.'

'What? Get away with yourself, man.'

'Seriously,' Harry said, not wanting to go into any details.

'Oh boy, are you blind or what?'

Harry smiled as McLeod read out his phone number then Harry did the same.

'You know exactly what I mean. The way she looks at you?'

'Honest, she's just sleeping in my spare room while work gets done on her own flat.'

'Christ, you really do mean it, don't you?'

'Of course I do, Dan.'

'Well, that lassie never got the message. If you were to ask my opinion, she's head over heels for you, boy.'

Harry could feel his face going red. 'Get over yourself.'

McLeod laughed. 'A blind man can see that.'

'Anyway, give me a call. I'm working a case right now, but I'll be around.'

'Good man. It will be good to catch up with old times.'

'It will indeed. Now, how much do I owe you?'

'Are you daft?' McLeod said. 'The meter's not even on.'

'You have to make a living, Dan. Come on, let me give you something.'

'Buy me a pint. That'll do.'

'You're some boy, let me tell you.'

'I'm looking forward to catching up,' McLeod said.

Harry opened the door letting the cold air in. As he stepped out, his phone rang.

'It's me,' Alex said. 'We've no milk for the coffee.'

He looked up at the window and saw her standing there, phone pressed to her ear, waving at him.

'Keep the kettle warm. I'll be ten minutes.'

He hung up, waved to McLeod, and walked round to the main road and along to Waitrose. Ten minutes had turned into twenty by the time he got back.

Upstairs, Alex had changed into her sleepwear, with flannel jimjams and her dressing gown.

'I remember the days when I had Robbie Evans' energy,' Harry said, taking the carrier bag through to the kitchen. Alex followed and reheated the kettle. Harry watched her and thought about what Dan McLeod had said; *She's head over heels for you, boy*.

Was she? Yes, they had a good time together, but did it go that far for Alex? No. She was selling her flat and she would be moving out soon.

'Dan seems nice,' she said.

'He is. He's a good guy. We got on really well, then I didn't see him much when I went into Standards.'

'Ah. Decaf?' she asked.

'Please. I feel knackered and I want to get a good night's sleep.'

She laughed. 'Ten years ago, I would have been going up the town, dancing and drinking until five. Now look at me; in my comfies and it's not even eleven.'

'And here's me, about to get changed and go out to a nightclub.'

She stopped. 'Are you really?'

'It's a toss-up between that and Netflix.'

'I'll look for a good movie for us to watch then, shall I?'

'Go ahead. I'll go get my slippers on.'

ELEVEN

The next morning, the big four-by-four was waiting downstairs for Harry and Alex. The sky was painted a dark grey and it had decided to throw more white stuff down to earth.

'The boy's upset the hotel didn't have a gym,' Jimmy Dunbar said as Harry and Alex climbed into the back.

'Hardly upset, boss,' Robbie Evans said.

'You should be like me; I only break a sweat in the morning when I can't decide between fried eggs or scrambled.'

'There's a crash cart at the Royal with your name on it. The old fart cart, we call it.' Evans grinned.

'Shut up,' Dunbar said. 'It's just gone ten and already you're doing my melon in. Just concentrate on getting out to this place without sticking this thing on its roof.'

They made small talk going along Queensferry Road, Alex giving Evans directions.

'I spoke to my DI last night. Good bloke. Has tremendous respect for the man who writes his annual report.' He threw a sideways glance at Evans, who was busy concentrating and pretending he was deaf. 'He's been authorised for overtime, along with one of my other crew. They're going to interview Christine Farr's family again today. But one interesting little nugget came up.'

There was silence for a moment as they headed round the Gogar roundabout.

'The suspense is killing me, Jimmy,' Harry said as the new tram depot slid by on their right.

'Sorry, pal, my life flashed before my eyes there,' he said as an airport bus came up from the roundabout underpass.

'You've had worse car rides on a Friday night when we've had to pour you into a taxi,' Evans said without taking his eyes off the road.

'More concentrating, less yapping,' Dunbar said and turned to face Harry. 'This woman we're going to have a chat with, Andrea Mann?'

'What about her?' Harry said.

'She was one of Christine Farr's bridesmaids at her wedding. There's our connection right there.'

'And now a woman who was killed in the same way is placed at her house. They know more than they're letting on,' Harry said.

Five minutes later, they made it to the road leading to Kellerstain Stables guesthouse.

'This is a nice wee bit of the country. Better than sucking in the fumes in the middle of Auld Reekie, eh?' Dunbar said, getting out of the big car.

'It certainly is. You should bring the wife through here one day, Jimmy.'

'Maybe when there's a better than fifty per cent chance of the sun coming out.'

The forensics tent was still in place, the big BMW car parked across the road. Other police vehicles were there, including the forensics vans. DI Maggie Parks, head of forensics, was walking across to them, almost ghostlike in her white forensic suit. They were wearing red reflective bands round their arms.

'This is DCI Jimmy Dunbar, and his colleague, DS Robbie Evans.'

'Good to meet, DI Parks,' Dunbar said, shaking her hand.

'Call me Maggie.'

Dunbar turned to Evans. 'That doesn't include you.'

'Ma'am,' Evans said, shaking her hand.

'Do we have anything, Maggie?' Harry asked.

'Nothing much to go on here. Whoever dumped her, obviously had to have transport, but the snow has come down so thick and fast that it covered any tracks. We've asked that nobody leave the guesthouse until they've been interviewed by yourselves. They're in the house now with Mr and Mrs Corbett.'

'We'll talk to them after we have a chat with the Manns,' Harry said.

Inside, they found Hector Mann and his wife in the living room with their children and a Family Liaison Officer, a young woman who was there mainly to stop the parents escaping the kids.

'Mr and Mrs Mann, I'd like to introduce DCI Dunbar from Police Scotland Glasgow Division, and his colleague, DS Evans.'

A look passed between the couple, like they knew why Dunbar was there.

'Can we sit down?' Harry said when nobody moved. He eyed the leather settee, wondering if he should give the Glasgow contingent a heads-up that a little boy had attempted to give the furniture a destruction test the day before, but left it.

He sat on a chair while the others found seats.

The boy in question came running into the living

room like the rest of the house was on fire, followed by his sister who was walking at a slower pace.

'I want breakfast!' Callum shouted at the top of his voice. His hair was in disarray and he wasn't wearing any slippers.

'Callum, these people are police officers,' Andrea Mann said, an edge to her voice. More interest would have been shown if the detectives were wearing Santa outfits, but such as it was, his mother was merely hindering him from eating and watching cartoons.

'Hello, young man,' Dunbar said. Callum mumbled something and Dunbar quickly shot Harry a look when he thought the little boy had suggested his parents weren't married. Harry shrugged.

'Get across to the table and I'll put toast on,' Hector Mann said. 'What flavour of jam do you want?'

The boy ran over to the table and Harry couldn't make out if he was telling his father his favourite flavour or whether he had just insulted him.

'Currant it is then,' Hector said, walking through to the kitchen.

'We only have strawberry,' Andrea said, looking puzzled.

'Maybe you should do it,' Hector said, frazzled.

'Sit down, Mr Mann,' Dunbar said. 'We need to talk to you. And your wife when she's finished with the toaster.'

'Have you identified the woman yet?' he asked. His face looked drawn like sleep had eluded him.

'Have you heard the name Mhari Baxter before?'

They heard a clatter from the kitchen as a plate fell to the floor and smashed into a thousand pieces. Andrea came rushing back in. 'Mhari?' she said.

'Yes,' Dunbar said. 'Her identity was confirmed yesterday.'

'We know that you knew Christine Farr,' Alex said.

Andrea sat down beside her husband. 'Good God, first Christine and now Mhari. Were they killed by the same person?'

'That's what we're trying to ascertain,' Harry said.

'Where's my toast?' Callum shouted.

'I'll get it,' the FLO said, walking through to the kitchen.

'Let's start by getting some background on how you knew the two women,' Dunbar said.

Hector Mann sat staring like he'd seen a ghost. 'We all met at university,' he said. 'There was a group of us. We hung out, went drinking together and had the same classes.'

'What classes were they?'

'Engineering and architecture. Some of us went more into the engineering field, but a couple of us went into architecture.'

'We need to know why somebody would kill Mhari

and put her in your driveway, and leave her the way he did,' Harry said.

'I have no idea.' Mann shook his head.

'Have either of you received threats from anybody?'

'I haven't.' Mann looked at his wife. 'Have you?'

She shook her head. 'No. But like we mentioned yesterday, we reported somebody creeping about here. Maybe it was the killer, checking us out.' She looked over at the kids, who were sitting at the table, waiting on toast that the FLO wasn't making fast enough.

Dunbar looked at Evans. 'Go and call DI Forbes and ask him to look into Christine Farr's background, see if she made any complaints about somebody following her or spying on her. Stuff like that.'

'Yes, sir,' Evans said and got up and left the room.

'Have either of you heard of Roger Pollock?' Dunbar asked.

They both shook their heads. 'Who is he?' Mann asked.

'He was reported to the police by Christine. He was harassing her at work, and she thought he was following her home. He had an alibi when she was murdered.'

'People have been known to hire other people to kill for them, and then be far away with an airtight alibi,' Andrea said. The three remaining detectives looked at her.

'What?' she said to her husband. 'I watch those real-life crime shows.'

'What, to get some ideas?' Mann said.

'Yeah. My favourite is *Wives with knives*.'

'That's not even funny.' Mann scowled.

'Cow,' Callum said from the table, obviously thinking his father was going to follow through with an insult.

'Callum! That's enough, for God's sake,' Mann said. 'I think he watches too much TV.'

Andrea looked at her husband like she wished she had a knife in her hand right now.

'There wasn't any evidence that Roger Pollock was guilty of murdering Christine,' Dunbar said. 'He was a pest, by all accounts, nothing more.'

'Why was Mhari staying at Kellerstain?' Harry asked.

Mann looked unsure for a moment. 'She was here to discuss the possibility of going into partnership with us and the others.'

'What sort of business?' Alex asked.

'She was an interior designer. We were going to invest in old properties. You know, buy them cheap, do them up, then flip them for a decent profit. We get together now and again, to catch up with old times, and this year, I suggested we at least think about going into business together. You know, buy something cheap, then work our way up to buying Balmoral Castle.'

'This is no time to be flippant,' Andrea said.

'I'm just trying to illustrate a point. Start off small, get bigger by ploughing the money back into the properties.'

The FLO came in with a plate of toast and put it down in front of the children. 'Is that okay?' she asked.

'Yes, thanks,' Callum said. 'Mummy usually makes our toast black but she scrapes it with a knife over the sink. This brown toast is better.'

The FLO tried not to laugh as she spread some jam on the toast.

'There are a lot of sharks in the construction business,' Dunbar said. 'I've had dealings with plenty of them in Glasgow, and if you come from there, you'll know what I'm talking about.'

'I wouldn't know about that,' Mann said. 'We come from Edinburgh, but the others were from Glasgow.'

'Do you know where we can contact them?'

Harry looked at him. 'They're up the road in the guesthouse. I spoke to the owners yesterday.'

TWELVE

'I believe you are all friends with Hector Mann?' Harry said, facing the group of people. There was only one man, and he assumed and had confirmed that this was Charlie Henderson. Amber Dodds, Rose Ashland and Lane Mott each introduced themselves.

'Tea or coffee?' Cat Corbett said, coming into the conservatory dining room. The general consensus was that they would like coffee. Harry and Dunbar sat at a dining table opposite the small group.

'I'm sorry but we have some bad news,' Harry said, loosening his jacket.

'That was Mhari, wasn't it?' Henderson said.

'It was, yes.'

Henderson was in his early thirties, with thinning hair on top. The others were a similar age, which would fit in with what Hector Mann had said about them all going to university at the same time.

'When's the last time any of you saw Mhari?' Dunbar said.

It was starting to snow outside again, coming down heavily, landing on the panes of glass on the top of the conservatory.

There was a general mumbling, like they were trying to get their story straight.

'Tuesday night,' the slim, petite, short-haired, Amber said.

'Mr Mann said you're all here to consider buying into property, is that right?' Harry said.

'Yes,' Henderson answered. 'We met up a few years ago after we caught up on Facebook, and when we were having a meal, somebody suggested we should pool our resources and start buying places to flip. We all have a talent that we can bring to the table.'

Rose looked at him and he shut up. 'Some of us are architects, some are designers. We can make a killing,' she said, then Harry saw her cheeks blush at her unfortunate turn of phrase.

'Did Mhari say where she was going?' Dunbar asked.

'She was going to meet somebody,' Lane said.

'Who?'

'She didn't say. All she said was, it was an old

friend and it was somebody who could help us. She drove herself.'

'And you've no idea who this could be?' Dunbar said, not convinced.

'I just said so, didn't I?'

'Did any of you report her missing?' Harry said.

Cat brought the coffee pot in and grabbed some mugs from the Welsh dresser over on one side. She came back with some milk in a jug. Sugar packets were on each table.

'None of us did, that I know of,' Henderson said. 'Mhari was the life and soul of the party. I personally thought she'd met up with an old boyfriend or something.'

Harry poured two coffees, and gave one to Dunbar.

'She leaves, what... Tuesday night? Is that right?'

'Yes,' Rose answered softly. 'Tuesday evening around seven.'

'The next thing you know, it's Friday morning and Mhari's been covered in snow and she's put in front of the driveway of your friend. Just down the road. And none of you knows anything,' Dunbar said. 'Excuse me if I find this a bit incredulous, but your friend goes out in a snowstorm, doesn't return and you lot think it's business as usual? Do I look like my head's buttoned up the back?'

'Now listen here—' Henderson began, standing up.

'Sit down,' Dunbar ordered, and his tone of voice suggested that he shouldn't be argued with. Henderson's face went red and he sat back down.

'Why choose this place to stay?' Harry asked.

'Hector told us about it. He said it would be a lot easier if we stayed here so we could meet easily,' Rose said.

Dunbar still wasn't happy. 'You're the only guests here, but nobody discussed what Mhari was up to or who she was seeing?'

They looked at each other and then back at the DCI.

'She wasn't being held prisoner here,' Henderson said.

Dunbar stood up and walked out of the conservatory.

Harry also stood and finished his coffee. Left one of his business cards on the table. 'If any of you remember anything, give me a call. And think on this; Christine Farr was murdered two years ago. Now one of her friends was murdered in the same way. Two years apart, just think about it. This guy knows how to keep a grudge. And maybe he's not finished.'

He walked out to find Dunbar standing talking to Cat in the hallway.

'The guests just come over to have breakfast in the

conservatory. The rooms are out in the old stable block.'

'And you never heard Mhari Baxter saying where she was going Tuesday night?' Dunbar was saying.

'No. She left in her car and she hasn't been back.'

'Thanks. You've been a great help. And when forensics have finished going through her room, we'd like to have a look.'

'That's fine. If I can be of any help at all, please give me or Ed a shout. This is horrible.' She walked away into her own living room and closed the door behind her.

'I wonder what she would be thinking if she knew that one of that lot could be a raving axe murderer,' Harry said.

'I think they might very well get booted out on their ear.' He smiled. 'What did you think of my performance in there? You think I had them worried?'

'You had *me* worried.'

'They're at it, Harry. You and I have been round the block more than a few times, and they've concocted some story about Mhari going to meet somebody.'

'I agree. They're definitely up to something.'

They walked out into the driving snow.

'I hope young Evans is behaving with my sergeant,' Harry said.

'I think she might have him in a headlock by now. If she hasn't already ripped a body part off.'

'You like Evans?'

'He's a clown at times, Harry, but a few months ago, a couple of bastards nearly got the better of me in a boozer. Robbie set about them. Battered four of them. I owe the wee arsehole.' He grinned. 'Aye, he's a good laddie to have on your side. What about Alex?'

'Same. I was a pariah when I left Standards. She was being given a hard time by my predecessor. We get on like a house on fire.'

'And she's living with you now.'

'She rents a room. But how did you find out?'

'It's the worst kept secret, Harry.'

'We're just friends...' Harry started to say, before Dunbar put up a hand.

'Like I said to those reprobates in there; do you think my heid's buttoned up the back?'

'It's true, Jimmy. We're just good friends.'

Dunbar grinned. 'You know what that river in Egypt's called, don't you?'

'What?'

'Denial.'

THIRTEEN

The forensics crew had been thorough with Mhari Baxter's room. Fingerprint dust was everywhere. DI Maggie Parks met the senior detectives in the room after they called her to join them. They wore overshoes as they stepped inside.

'As you can see, we dusted everything and we'll run all the prints through the system, but it's going to take a while to get results, if any. I mean, she could have had somebody in here without the owner of the guesthouse knowing. But anybody could have come in.'

'You mean like Edwin Corbett?' Dunbar said, looking around.

'I mean like anybody, sir, if she had a mind. Maybe she was expecting to have a man round. Or a woman. I don't know what her sexual preferences were.'

'We're going on the theory that a man was responsible,' Harry said. 'Although not ruling out a female being a possibility.'

'I know, sir,' Maggie said. 'The rules of probability, and all that.'

'Find anything interesting in her belongings?' Dunbar asked.

'Yesterday we looked for her phone but it wasn't on her. It hasn't been found in here either.'

'Her car is gone too. Nobody's seen it since she left.'

The room was large, with a double bed against one wall, a little table with two chairs off to one side, and a small couch behind it. A vanity with a chair in front of it sat opposite the bed, with a set of drawers next to it. A door led into a private bathroom.

Harry started looking through the drawers and found some pamphlets from the Scottish Tourist Board, something that Cat Corbett might have left in the room for guests to have a browse through.

In amongst them was a small Christmas card. It wasn't shop bought, somebody had had it made up professionally by taking a photo and having it made into cards. There was no company name on the back but there was the name of a printer at the bottom. It showed a tree decorated with Christmas lights. And a snowman standing next to it.

Harry took out his phone and snapped a photo.

'What you got there?' Dunbar asked.

'It's a Christmas card. Something somebody had made up at one of those printers who do business cards.'

Dunbar looked at it. 'I wonder why anybody would go to all the trouble? I've seen better from Marks and Sparks.'

'It must mean something to somebody, Jimmy. I mean, let's say I wanted to have a photo taken with an ugly sweater on, then I might want to have it made into a card.'

'I suppose.'

'But have a look at this,' Harry said. He put the card down and opened up the photos on his phone. Zoomed in a bit.

'What am I looking at here, Harry?'

'The look on the snowman's face; somebody made him a brow and it's furrowed, like he's not happy to be there. Like he's scowling. Not a friendly snowman at all. And look at his front.'

'Three red buttons,' Dunbar said as Harry moved the photo down.

'Almost like three stab wounds.'

'And Mhari Baxter was stabbed.'

'Three times. Just like our snowman there.'

FOURTEEN

'The trouble and strife lets you out on a Saturday afternoon to get blootered with the mates? She's a keeper, Ian.' The man smiled.

Ian Wallace didn't. 'Shut up. I didn't ask you out to take the piss.' He chugged back his pint.

'You have it good, mate. Don't knock it.' Kevin Shearing drank his own pint at a slower pace.

Wallace knocked his back and wiped his mouth with the back of his hand. 'Same again?'

Shearing looked at his own glass, still three-quarters full. 'Maybe a wee nip.'

Wallace turned to the barman. There were a fair number of people in the St Bernard's in Stockbridge, his old local.

'Does Stella know you're down here?'

Wallace turned back with the two drinks. 'I really don't give a toss. She booted me into touch weeks ago.'

'That's not what Alex thinks, is it?'

'I told her that so she wouldn't think I'm a loser. I don't even have a girlfriend, never mind a fucking wife and daughter.'

'I don't see why you're bothered so much. I mean, she's selling the house and you'll get money off it.'

'Hardly enough to start over. Have you seen the house prices recently?' Wallace took a healthy chug of his pint.

'Now Alex will be in the same boat; she won't have the flat either.'

'She doesn't have to worry though, does she? She's moved in with Mr Big Shot.'

'She's moved on. Like you should do, mate.'

'Christ, it was a one-night stand. I mean, it's not as if I fell in love with the woman.'

'You're talking about the woman you cheated on Alex with?'

'Of course I am. She was a fling. A meaningless fling, but Alex didn't see it that way.' Wallace was feeling more and more angry by the minute.

'How's the job front looking?'

'Who wants to hire a drunken ex-firefighter who was fired for drinking on the job? And the only reason I started drinking during the day was because of my relationship with Alex.'

'You can't blame her, Ian.'

'Can't I? If she had just overlooked my little indiscretion, I would have still been living with her and I still would have been a firefighter. Now she's got that copper to keep her warm at night.'

His friend finished his pint and knocked back the nip. 'So what are you going to do now?'

'You'll see, buddy. You'll see.'

The police HQ building at Fettes was quiet with it being Saturday, but not quite deserted. Harry was gathered with the other officers in their offices. He'd called in his team, DS Eve Bell, DI Karen Shiels and DC Simon Gregg.

'As you all know, a young woman was murdered and covered in snow yesterday,' Harry said after making the introductions. 'Killed in the same way as Christine Farr two years ago through in Glasgow. It turns out that the group who are staying up at Kellerstain knew Christine. That's why I asked you, Eve, to do some background work on them. If we could go over that now.'

Eve stood up and walked over to the whiteboard.

'The three of us were working on the background this morning. And I'd like to start off with Hector Mann.' She tapped a photo of the man that had been stuck to the board.

'Hector Mann is thirty-two, married to Andrea for the past eight years. They met in uni in Glasgow, just like he said. He's an architect with Hume and Colson, a big firm here in Edinburgh. He's working on the new St James Centre, on Leith Street. That all ties in with what he told you, sir.

'But you told me he also said he and the others are planning on getting together to buy property to invest in. And this is where it gets a bit shaky.'

Karen Shiels stepped up beside her. 'Basically, the Manns are in tremendous debt.'

'That house they live in must be worth a pretty penny,' Dunbar said.

'It is, sir. I checked. It's worth over half a mil. But Hector Mann doesn't own it.'

'Who does?' Harry asked.

'Edwin Corbett. He owns all the properties on that land. The other house is rented out too, but it's empty just now, except for the housekeeper. The renter is an American professor and his wife. Two kids. They're in America, visiting his mother who's dying. They've been away for a week, so they weren't even here when the murder happened.'

'But Mann pays rent, I assume?' Alex said.

'We got a warrant for his financial records,' Karen said, 'and he has very little in the bank, but it shows he pays fifteen hundred a month rent, plus his bills so as soon as his salary hits his bank account, it goes straight out again.'

'Is it a joint account with his wife?' Evans asked.

'Yes. She works as a designer. She owns her agency, and does a lot of work from home. Brings in more money than he does, but there are a lot of bookies' accounts on their bank statements. Money is flying in and out of there every day.'

'He's a big gambler, then,' Simon Gregg said.

'It would seem like that. One of them is, for sure, but we're assuming it's him. And by all accounts, he loses more often than he wins, and his pay goes to the horses as well.'

'Maybe they're all clubbing together to try and buy a property like they said. Start off small, then work their way up with the profits,' Dunbar said.

'That would be a reasonable assumption, sir, until we look at the financial records for the others. They all earn good money, but they're all in debt.'

Harry leaned back in the office chair. 'Basically, that was a load of flannel they told us about investing in property.'

'I would say so,' Karen replied.

'If they haven't got a pot to piss in, then what are they really up to?' Dunbar said.

'What profession was Christine Farr in?' Alex asked.

Dunbar looked at Evans.

'She was an engineer,' Evans said. 'She worked for a firm in Glasgow city centre. Divorced. Nothing stuck out when we ran her background again. But some of our team back home are delving deeper.'

'It was two years ago when she was taken,' Harry said, 'in a snowstorm. That's no coincidence.'

'Show them the photo,' Dunbar said.

Harry took his phone out and they came to have a look.

'It was a Christmas card that Mhari Baxter had in her room. It has red buttons down the front, just like she had stab wounds on her front. Let's find out the connection.'

FIFTEEN

'Were you not comfortable inviting Jimmy and Robbie over for dinner?' Alex asked.

'I did invite them, but Jimmy wanted to have a conference call with his DI.'

'Is he still going for a pint with you and Dan McLeod?'

'He is. To be honest, I thought Dan would have wanted to be out and about on a Saturday night. It's one of the biggest nights of the week for a cabbie.'

Alex stood looking out of the window. 'Look at the weather; I don't think this is going to be a busy night.' She turned back to face him. 'I hope Jimmy and Robbie don't think I can't stand up for myself. After what happened with Ian last night.'

Harry walked over to her. 'Of course not. I just asked them to come along for backup and also to be witnesses. The way you were acting, I knew you were worried how he'd act, and I thought there was a good chance he was going to come along with some of his pals.'

'I don't think he has any pals left. He's a big drinker. That's what got him the sack from his job.'

'I don't think you'll have any problem from him from now on. And if you do, you know you just have to tell me and we can have it taken care of.'

'I hope he was just talking out of anger when he said this isn't over.'

'I've been threatened more times than I can remember. Don't worry about him.'

She looked at him for a moment. 'I do worry. That's why I've made the decision to move out.'

Harry didn't know what to say for a moment. 'You don't have to do that. He's not a threat to me.'

'It's not fair on you, Harry. You've been good to me letting me stay here.'

'It's no problem.'

'I know it's not. But I'm just being stupid. I have a perfectly good flat just along the road and here I am, spending time in your flat.'

He put his hands on her arms, more so that she wouldn't see his hands shaking. 'You don't have to do this.'

She reached a hand up and gently stroked his

cheek. 'I really do. For more reasons than you'll ever know, Harry McNeil.'

She walked away from him and went through to her own room, gently closing the door behind her.

Harry got ready and called Dan first, just to make sure he was still up for a pint. He explained about Jimmy Dunbar and suggested they could meet in the bar of the hotel where Jimmy was staying.

'Sounds good to me, Harry. I'll leave for a bus shortly.'

'A cabbie getting a bus?' Harry said, laughing.

'It's cheaper,' McLeod said. 'I won't give those robbing bastards a single penny.' He laughed as he hung up.

'Must be like working in a bakery and not wanting to eat another pie,' Harry said out loud.

He looked at his watch. It was getting close to eight o'clock. The snow was again covering everything in the darkness outside. He felt happy, going to see his old friend again, but then he thought of Alex and that twat she had been going to marry. He reckoned she'd had a lucky escape.

He walked through to her room and gently knocked. 'I'm going out to meet Jimmy and Dan now. You want to come along?'

'No, I'll be fine, thanks,' she said through the door.

It sounded like she was crying again. He could understand why; Ian Wallace had been a big part of her life for so long until he had betrayed her. He wondered if Alex was sad for a future that would never come, or for a past that had been destroyed. Neither was a winner.

He grabbed his red coat from the hall cupboard. He didn't want to look like he was going to work.

Downstairs, he stopped outside the stair door to talk to his next door neighbour, Mia.

'Away out on your own on a Saturday night, Harry?' she said. 'What about Alex?'

'We don't go everywhere together,' Harry replied.

'Since when?' She grinned at him.

'She's just my roommate, you know that.'

'Let me put it this way; if she's not your girlfriend now, you should discuss things with her pretty soon. I've seen the way she looks at you. She wants to be your girlfriend more than anything.'

'You're a blether.'

She kept smiling. 'You might be a detective, Harry, but I'm a woman. Have a good night now.'

He stood still for a moment. The snow kept falling so he pulled up the hood on his coat. Why was everybody else seeing things that he didn't?

Because you're a gentleman, Harry.

He crossed the road to Comely Bank Place and

walked round by the mews houses, coming out opposite the hotel. Dirty buses splashed by. Pedestrians huddled against the snow.

Harry made it across the road into the hotel where Jimmy Dunbar was waiting in the bar.

All cried out, Alex came out of her room after hearing Harry leave the flat. She had meant what she said about leaving. How could she even begin to carry on living here when she felt like she did? They had never shared a bedroom, and hadn't done anything together in that sense, but that only served to make her feelings even stronger.

The flat was warm, but she felt cold inside. She'd known Ian would be a prick, and that was why she had asked Harry along. But wasn't it more than that? Didn't she want to rub it in Ian's face that she had moved on, and now she was dating a terrific man? Yes, she did, even though she and Harry weren't dating.

She had kissed him under the mistletoe on Christmas day, but it hadn't gone any further, although God knows she wouldn't have stopped him if he'd tried anything. But Harry was too much of a gentleman. A little old-fashioned, but then she remembered he had been hurt too. His first marriage had gone down the tubes, but as far as he knew, his first wife hadn't cheated on him, and he swore he hadn't cheated on her either, they had just drifted apart.

She pulled her dressing gown tighter around herself.

She wished Harry were here right now, but she wasn't his wife, or his girlfriend, so she had no right to ask him to stay in. Not that she would have wanted to even if they were married, but she just wanted him to be here right now.

Harry was out with his friends, and she knew she would never stop him from going out even if they were together. She just missed him. What with her staying here and working together, they were with each other practically twenty-four hours a day. But what if he didn't feel the same way about her?

She didn't want to make a fool of herself. She'd have to quit her job and move away.

Alex walked over to the window and looked out into the darkness, keeping the lights off. She saw Harry walking on the other side of the road, at the corner of the bowling club, his red jacket sticking out a mile. He went out of sight for a moment, then reappeared further up the road where he stopped opposite Vanessa's house.

This was another factor in how she felt about him;

Vanessa. He obviously held a candle for her. Why else would he be standing opposite her house?

She turned away from the window. She'd never felt so confused in her whole life.

She went back to her room and climbed into bed.

SIXTEEN

Vanessa Harper had thought about the invitation to go drinking with some of the teachers from the nursery she owned, but had decided against it. They really did want her to go out with them but tonight she just wanted to stay in and watch some Netflix.

She wondered what Harry was doing. Then she mentally kicked herself. He had moved on, and so should she. If only the fake boyfriend she'd tried to make Harry jealous with was her real one.

Her living room curtains were open again. She kept the light off in the front room, so she could see out. The darkness beyond the window wasn't quite as dark as it had been since the snow had covered everything. It reflected the light and made everything easier to see.

Including the man standing watching her window.

He was wearing a red jacket this time, and a black scarf covering his face. Black gloves too.

She should have gone to the police about getting the postcard with the hangman on it, but they would have laughed at her. Now she was shaking as her hand reached for her telephone. She would call the police now.

And tell them what?

There's a strange man standing outside my house on the other side of the road. Standing watching my house. No, he's not doing anything threatening.

Just imagining the conversation with the operator was making her feel foolish. What if it was just a man walking his dog? She wouldn't see the dog for the cars parked across there.

Should she just shut the curtains now?

The man turned away and started walking down the hill.

God, Vanessa, you are a stupid cow, she thought, just as the snowball came crashing against her window.

She yelped and jumped back. Did he see her after all? She ducked and saw the man still walking down the hill, but he kept looking over his shoulder at her. Then he walked past the bowling club and turned right into Harry's street.

She closed the curtains but left the light out then went into the hallway and saw the envelope sitting on the floor. When did that come in? Maybe the man in red had put it there, through her letterbox, before standing in front of her house.

She walked towards it and picked it up. It wasn't sealed. Inside was a letter. She took it out and unfolded it.

There were letters stuck to it, just like ransom notes she had seen in films and on TV.

She read the words over and over.

You'll pay for what you did they said. Different colours and sizes, but they all combined to deliver the message.

Was Harry responsible for this? It had to be him.

Well, he wasn't going to frighten her. She would call somebody first thing Monday morning. She would make sure he was the one who paid.

SEVENTEEN

'Robbie not coming down for a beer?' Harry said, putting a pint in front of Jimmy Dunbar. He sat down beside him at a table.

'Get this, the wee arsehole is away out on the lash. I told him he could have a night off and he took full advantage of the situation. But it is Saturday night.'

'He's a good lad,' Harry said.

'Aye, he is, just don't tell him that.' Dunbar raised his glass in salute. 'Where's your pal?'

'He'll be here shortly. He's getting the bus.'

'I thought he drove a taxi?'

'He does. He's just a tight wad.'

'I don't blame him. When I want a lift home, I call one of our own taxis with the wee blue lights on the roof.' He smiled. 'But Standards wouldn't have looked too kindly on that, eh?'

'I never investigated anybody for doing that. It would be a poor show if we pulled in a senior detective for that. But no matter what I say, some coppers will never trust me again.'

Dunbar laughed. 'Fuck 'em, Harry. You're a good detective, so what does it matter what anybody else thinks?'

'True. That's why I was glad to bump into Dan. He's a good guy.'

'And you never investigated him, I assume?'

'You assume correctly.'

Just then, the door opened and in walked Dan. 'Damn bus was late,' he said, shaking the smattering of snow off his head. Luckily, the bus stop was right outside the hotel.

'You should have got a taxi,' Harry said, standing up and making the introductions.

'They're all rip-off merchants,' he said, laughing. 'Good to meet you, Jimmy.'

'Harry tells me you were in the force too,' Dunbar said after Harry had brought more drinks.

'I was indeed. Ten years in CID, but then I decided it was getting too stifling. I didn't like the way things were going, so I got out.'

'God knows what the future is going to bring,' Dunbar said. 'I personally can't see the benefit of us being one big force. Everybody thought it was so they could make cuts a lot easier.'

'To be honest, I miss the job, but I don't miss the aggravation. Don't get me wrong, I still get hassle. But I'm my own boss.'

'As long as you're happy, mate.'

'How's Margo doing?' Harry asked.

McLeod hung his head for a moment before looking Harry in the eyes. 'You didn't hear?'

Harry looked unsure for a moment. 'Hear what?'

McLeod took in a breath and let it out slowly. 'It was three years ago now. Almost to the day. She died in a car crash. Out on the bypass.'

Harry was speechless for a moment. 'Christ, Dan, I hadn't heard.'

'No matter. Time's a healer, eh?' He took a drink with a shaky hand. Then he gave a small, humourless laugh. 'Listen to me; Danny downer. Bringing the whole conversation to its knees. What a choob. Let me get some nips in. Whisky okay?'

They agreed it was.

'God Almighty, talking about putting my foot in it,' Harry said.

'You weren't to know, mate,' Dunbar said. 'It's not your fault.'

A few minutes later McLeod sat back down.

'Listen, Dan, I'm sorry about Margo.'

'Harry, don't worry about it. I've spoken to other

people who hadn't heard. It's not a big deal. We had twenty good years together. I miss her every day, but life goes on. Cheers.'

They clinked glasses and talked about the old days, comparing notes about policing in Glasgow versus Edinburgh.

Dunbar reckoned that Edinburgh coppers were just Glasgow coppers with their brains bashed in.

At that moment in time, Harry didn't disagree.

EIGHTEEN

It wasn't too late when Harry got home. Jimmy Dunbar had gone up to his room while Dan went out to catch a bus home. Harry stood in the bus shelter waiting with him where they'd exchanged a few anecdotes and promised to keep in touch so they could have another drink sometime.

He put the kettle on and thought about knocking on Alex's door to see if she wanted a cuppa, but didn't bother. She might be sleeping.

But what if she's gone?

She was neither, he discovered when she came into the kitchen. 'A nice cuppa would go down a treat,' she said.

'Decaf?'

'That depends.'

'On what?' he said turning to look at her.

'Whether I'm staying or not. I might need the caffeine to keep me going when I'm hauling my stuff downstairs.'

'Listen, you don't have to go anywhere. I know this business with Ian has you rattled, but there's no need for you to move out. I like having you here. I mean, you're a cheeky wee besom at times, but the alternative is getting a parrot. And they swear.'

'More than me?'

'Not more than you, no, but I would have to clean its cage out.'

She smiled and stepped closer to him. 'I'm going to say something here that might just blow our relationship out of the water, both personally and professionally, but I don't care. Staying silent would be remiss.'

'Look, if it's about you paying rent, I said you don't have to...'

'Shut up, Harry.'

'Yes, ma'am.' He made the tea and coffee and they went through to the settee where they put their mugs on the coffee table.

'When I first met you last summer, I told you the truth about me having no friends. I did have of course, but they dwindled when I became a police officer, then when you tell them you're in CID, they drift off. I sort of put my whole social life into Ian's and we would drink with his friends. It was good until we split. Then I was just going to work and having a drink with some colleagues. When you came into the cold case unit, I don't know, it's... we just made a connection. I felt something inside. Like we'd known each other forever. Does that make sense?'

'It does actually. I tried explaining that to Vanessa, that we were good friends, but she didn't want to hear about it.'

'You let me stay here after that guy was in my flat, and again when the decorators were in. There's no reason for me to be here anymore, but I'm comfortable. You make me feel safe, and you're a true friend. And that's where the problem lies.'

He sipped his coffee. 'Go on.'

'You've been a perfect gentleman. I know guys who would have tried it on a long time ago, but you respected me, and that's not common these days. So I'm going to throw this out there, and I know this is a fork in the road for me; I've decided to hand in my resignation first thing Monday morning. I'm going to apply to work in the Met, Harry.'

'What? Why?'

She took a breath and looked him right in the eyes. 'I can't live here anymore, I already told you that. And for one reason. I've crossed the line.'

'What do you mean?' Harry wished he had put a stiff whisky in his coffee.

'We're friends, but I've fallen in love with you. I've known it ever since I kissed you at Christmas.'

He looked at her, not saying anything, watching her about to get up off the settee, so he put a hand out and gently grabbed her arm.

'I know how you feel.'

She sat back down and looked at him. 'You do?'

'I've known for a while. When you asked if you could come back and stay while you had the decorators in doing up your flat, I can't begin to tell you how I felt. It was like Christmas all over again. I've fallen for you too, Alex, but I couldn't say anything. I didn't want to ruin our friendship. I was just happy to have you with me here.'

'What if I'd wanted to leave? If I bought my own place?'

'I would have plucked up the courage to tell you. Hell, maybe I wouldn't have been able to. But, thank God, you told me first.'

She leaned forward and kissed him.

When they parted, he held her hand. 'It's up to you of course, but you're welcome to stay here. We can start off like we're dating. I don't want to go from being friends to... you know...'

She smiled at him. 'I wouldn't have expected

anything else from you, Harry McNeil. Your mother brought up a good boy. Now I can finally get to meet her.'

'Let's not rush things. The woman has a frail ticker.'

'There is one thing I have to know though, Harry, before we embark on this.'

'What's that?'

She looked uncertain for a moment. 'I have to know that things are finally over between you and Vanessa.'

'You know they are. We've been over for months.'

'I had to ask because, well, I came out here when you left, and I was looking over at the bowling club, wondering if I would ever be setting foot in there again, when I saw you walk up the hill to Vanessa's house. I mean, I wasn't spying. I just saw your red jacket and then you stopped at her house and stood staring.'

Harry looked puzzled. 'That wasn't me.'

'It was just after you left.'

'Alex, I went left and cut through by the mews houses. Hand on my heart, that wasn't me.'

'Okay. I believe you. I don't want our relationship to start off on a bad foot.'

'It won't. I'll never lie to you. And I promise you that it's over between me and Vanessa. However, it begs one question.'

'What's that?'

'Who was that staring at Vanessa's house?'

NINETEEN

'I don't care,' Lane Mott said. 'After we find what we're looking for, we can all go home.'

They were all sitting in the conservatory. It was dark outside, the snow filling in the gaps. It blanketed the field beyond and it looked like they were on some far-flung research station in the North Pole.

They had kept the lights out, and if Cat Corbett had come in, they would say they were just sitting around chatting, with the lights out because it was so beautiful outside. But nobody had disturbed them.

'Somebody is taking exception to us crawling around that place, but we don't know who,' Charlie Henderson said. 'Or why.'

Rose Ashland curled her lip. 'I think we can hazard a guess as to why.'

Henderson rounded on her. 'You're wrong there.

How could he know? How? Give me the answer. And why? It has nothing to do with anyone else other than the people in this room.'

Rose sneered at him and turned away.

'Well, I'm going to have a look around,' Lane said.

'What if it's not there?' Henderson said, exasperated.

'It is. It's why Mhari died. Otherwise, why would he bother stopping us?'

'That makes sense,' Amber Dodds said. 'What we're looking for is still there. We just need to find it.'

Lane stood up. 'I want to go and look now. Who wants to come?'

None of them did.

Then Henderson changed his mind. 'I'll go. Safety in numbers after all.'

'That's it settled. We can spend all night poking and prodding around. If we think logically, there are only so many hiding places.'

'It's big, though.' Henderson looked perplexed.

'We have to think smarter,' Lane said. She looked scary when she was angry.

'What if he moved it after he killed Mhari?'

'Then we just keep looking. Christ's sake, Charlie, it's why we're all here. We all got the tour. We familiarised ourselves with the layout the other day. Do I have to think for everyone?'

Nobody argued with her.

'Right, if there are no more objections, I'd like to go now. The snow will make it easier to see, so we shouldn't have too much difficulty finding our way around.'

'If we're going, then we should go now. We'll take my car,' Henderson said, stopping short of insulting Lane's little French hatchback.

Outside, the snow was falling hard but the Subaru cut through the snow with ease. They went past the police vehicles still outside Hector Mann's house and a couple of disinterested police officers looked at them as they went by.

The road was tricky until they got down to the main A90 and then it was slippery but manageable.

'Don't you ever wish you'd taken a different fork in the road in life?' Henderson said as they took it easy along the main road behind a van.

'If you mean, do I wish I'd never met you, then yes.'

Henderson kept his eyes on the road straight ahead. He'd always known Lane Mott could be a cow at times, but that comment cut through to the quick. If he found what they were looking for then he would never have to clap eyes on the bitch again.

Further along, they came to the private drive they were looking for. The snow was thicker here. There were no tracks in the fresh drifts but once again, the four-wheel drive car handled it with ease.

They drove past the old gatehouse and under the small railway bridge, then the old building came into view.

The old hotel. A large For Sale sign faced them, nailed onto a wooden frame erected to support it. The sign was dirty now, having been up for a long time.

The windows on the ground floor had been boarded up after the first few instances of vandalism.

'We'd be better going round the back,' Henderson said, pointing past the entrance to the hotel. The door was kept locked. They knew that after their visit the other day.

'Boy, I'm sure glad I brought you along. I would never have guessed,' Lane said.

'Shut up. We're in this together, remember?'

Lane made a face but didn't say anymore. Henderson hooked a right into the overflow car park at the side of the hotel. A road led round to the back, where deliveries were made, but he drove carefully to the far end of the car park to where another road was. This led down to the old buildings, where staff had lived.

The road curved round to the right, the Subaru still sure-footed as it made its way through the deep snow. They came out into a courtyard, with another road leading out to their left. The staff houses were here, as well as a garage block and an old building where maintenance machinery was kept.

'I wasn't back here, back in the day,' Henderson said.

'That's a garage over there. And you can barely make out a set of tracks leading to it.'

Henderson leaned forward, looking out past the windscreen wipers batting the snow away. He couldn't see any tracks.

'You see them?' Lane asked.

'Yes,' he lied.

He drove forward, the headlight beams bouncing off the snow, and stopped in front of the garage doors. He kept the engine running as they stepped out, and they walked over to the double garage doors. Old wooden things that opened outwards. They could both see they had been opened recently, with the marks they had made in the snow, although it had mostly been filled in again.

They were unlocked. Henderson grabbed hold of one of the metal round handles on the left-hand door and turned it and pulled the door towards them. It opened far enough for them to see in before it stopped.

'Get your phone out,' Lane ordered. 'Get the light on.'

'Why don't you take a fucking chill pill? You're not

my boss, so shut your hole.' He nevertheless took his phone out and put the light on and shone it inside the garage.

'What do you see?'

'Mhari's car. It's right there.'

'So, she was here. I wonder if she parked it in here out of the way, or...'

'Let's get back into the hotel and have a look round there.'

Lane stepped back. 'Why don't you think it was hidden in one of these buildings back then? If Mhari's car is here, then maybe she started her search for it back here.'

Henderson looked at her. 'It would have been more difficult to move out of the hotel and across here.'

'Not if he belonged here. If he was moving it, and he lived here, then nobody would question him. Maybe if he had it in a wheelbarrow and was walking about with it. Covered and hidden of course. Plus, it was Christmas time, so it got dark early.'

Henderson thought about it for a second and what she said made sense. 'You're right. Let's see if we can get into the houses. Maybe there's a loose board or something. Let's check the one down there first.' He pointed to a boarded-up house across from the garage.

'You take that one. I'll look in the other one.'

'Split up?'

'What are you? Twelve? Big baby.' She managed her disdainful look again.

'Fine.' Henderson trudged off to the house at the far end of the small car park. There were no footprints there so he was sure that nobody had walked here within the last hour or so. Nobody would be waiting inside.

He looked at the windows. They were boarded up tight. He walked round the back and saw that the board covering the window in the back door was loose. He pulled it aside and reached in, unlocking the door.

Inside, it was cold but not as bad as outside. He still had the light from his phone on and shone it around. It was a kitchen. Nothing out of the ordinary. He moved through into a hallway and checked out the rooms on the ground floor. Old, musty furniture filled the rooms. He then started walking up the staircase, the stairs creaking. If anybody was upstairs waiting, they would know he was on his way.

The windows up here weren't boarded up. Obviously somebody wasn't bothered if the windows were used for target practise, but had only boarded up the lower floor to deter squatters.

There were three bedrooms up here, with old, mouldy beds and bedroom furniture. No sign that anybody had been here in a while.

Then he heard the scream, coming from outside.

He ran downstairs, back out the way he'd come and round to the front of the house.

Lane was lying face down in the snow in front of the garage. He knelt down beside her and started shaking her shoulder.

'Hello, Charlie,' the voice said behind him. He spun his head round just in time to see the figure bring the metal bar down on his head.

TWENTY

Sunday was spent talking, getting to know each other better, even more than they had before. They ate dinner at a little bistro in Stockbridge, braving another storm, and Harry didn't touch alcohol.

'My liver needs a little rest,' he'd said.

Now, Monday morning had arrived and it was just like every other morning. He was drinking coffee in the living room, watching the news, by the time Alex had showered and come into the living room, dressed for work.

'Jimmy's coming round with the tank,' he said to her. 'Poor little Rory isn't getting to play in the snow again.'

'Keep on mocking why don't you? Then I can have a good laugh at what you decide to buy. Some girlie-mobile.'

'I want something with a little bit of class. Maybe I'll buy a classic Land Rover Defender.'

'So you want to walk to work, then?'

'Now, now. Those cars have been a British stalwart for many years.'

'So have buses, but I don't see you using them very often.'

'Nothing wrong with public transport. I don't partake because I have you to drive me around. Notice I didn't use the word *chauffeuse*?'

'Because that would have been sexist, and my new boyfriend doesn't want to put me off him.' She sat down beside him and gave him a kiss. 'You do find me attractive, don't you?'

'Of course I do. I wouldn't have told you my feelings if I didn't. I said I didn't want to rush things. I enjoyed our day together yesterday, getting to know each other better.'

'Me too.'

'Let me ask *you*; you find me attractive?'

'In a Quasi Modo kind of way.'

'The bells!' he said, doing a fair impression of Charles Laughton, who'd appeared in the 1939 classic.

Alex screamed and batted him away as he got closer to her. 'Be careful what you wish for,' he said, smiling as he went through to the kitchen for breakfast.

Half an hour later, Jimmy Dunbar honked the horn

and when Harry looked out, the police tank was waiting.

'See? That big police Land Rover can handle this kind of weather with ease.'

'So can a horse.'

'I see I'm going to have to whip you into shape.'

'Whip? And you carry handcuffs. I'm having doubts about you, Harry McNeil.'

'I'm a good kisser though.'

'Says who?'

'Come here,' he said, gently grabbing her and kissing her, only breaking when Jimmy Dunbar honked the horn again.

'Better not keep Jimmy waiting or else he'll send young Robbie up here to see what we're getting up to,' Harry said, grabbing his coat.

'As we discussed, we're keeping this between ourselves, yes?'

'Of course. One step at a time. As far as anybody knows, you're just renting out my room.'

They went downstairs and into the big off-road vehicle, where Dunbar and Evans were arguing over who was the harder man, The Rock, or Arnold Schwarzenegger.

'Bollocks, Arnie would belt the living daylights out of The Rock any day,' Dunbar said. 'Assuming we're talking about when Arnie was younger. If they were both the same age. Didn't you see the film *Commando*? Arnie was magic in that.'

'Don't talk pish, sir. The Rock is a machine.'

'So's a sausage-maker.'

'I know which one I would rather have on my side in a fight.'

'Away. Your bloody heid's a sausage-maker. Harry, back me up on this. Arnie or that big galloot, The Rock.'

'I prefer Bruce Willis myself.'

Evans pulled away from the side of the road.

'Away, man,' Dunbar said. 'Bruce Willis? Are you daft?'

'He was in the greatest Christmas movie ever. *Die Hard*.'

'Christ, what happened to *It's A Wonderful Life*?'

'Never seen it myself,' Alex said.

Harry and Dunbar looked at her. Speechless.

'I prefer Patrick Swayze,' she said. 'Haven't you boys ever seen *Dirty Dancing*?'

None of them admitted to having seen it.

'Sheltered lives. I bet young Robbie there has seen it.'

'*Sheltered Lives* or *Dirty Dancing*?'

Dunbar shook his head. 'You're asking the wrong bloke there. If the character doesn't have a gun in his hand, Robbie isn't interested. Isn't that right, son?'

'I know culture,' he replied, managing to sound offended.

'Going to the museum when you were a laddie doesn't count. And keep your bloody eyes on the road.'

Inside HQ, they were given a confirmation that Hector Mann had turned up for his interview, as requested.

Harry and Dunbar met him in one of the interview rooms, while the others were doing background checks in the incident room.

'Thank you for coming along here today,' Harry said.

'Have you caught him?' Mann said, gripping the polystyrene cup of coffee that sat on the table in front of him.

'We're good, son, but we're not that good. Unless he was standing over the body with a knife, of course,' Dunbar said.

'No surprise there, then,' Mann mumbled, lifting the cup to his mouth.

'Right, let's go over your relationship with Mhari Baxter and Christine Farr.'

'Hardly a relationship. Friendship. We were friends.'

'What about Christine?' Dunbar asked.

'She was part of our group. We stayed in touch, all

of us. Christine got married and my wife was her bridesmaid.'

'Did you ever go through to Glasgow to visit her?'

'Of course we did. Half of our group lives there.'

'When did you decide to embark on this venture of yours, flipping property?' Harry asked.

'We've been bouncing the idea around for a long time.'

'You said you were all going to invest money, but we have a copy of your financial records, and basically, you like to invest your money in the bookies, don't you, Mr Mann?'

Mann put the cup back on the table. 'I do enjoy a bet. Not against the law, is it?'

'Of course it isn't,' Dunbar said, leaning forward. 'But we're wondering why you were spouting all this stuff about putting money into old places when we can clearly see you're an addictive gambler.'

'We have money.'

'Where, Mr Mann? Where do you have money? Stuffed under your mattress?' Harry said. 'We've been through your financial records, and just to back it up, they're going to a forensic accountant, in case we missed something, but I don't think we did. Do you?'

'I was told I was here voluntarily. I can go at any time, can't I?'

'You can, Mr Mann. You can get up at any time

you like, but in case you haven't watched any real-life crime shows recently, as soon as you do that, you elevate yourself to number one person of interest.'

'Is that a threat?'

'You can take it any way you want.'

Mann shook his head. 'No matter what I say, you're going to think I did something to Mhari, and that is far from the case.'

'Help us find who did then,' Harry said.

'I don't know who harmed her. I don't know who killed Christine. And I've had enough of this. If you want to talk to me again, you can do it with my lawyer present.' He got up and stalked out of the interview room.

'What a stuck-up ponce,' Dunbar said. 'He knows something. They all do, Harry, and I want to know what. Let's get surveillance on him.'

'I'll arrange it.'

Up in the incident room, they were talking about Mann and his friends when two men in suits walked in. Nobody recognised them.

'Help you, pal?' Dunbar said.

The older man smiled at Dunbar but there was no warmth there.

'We're not here to talk to you, DCI Dunbar. We need to talk to DCI McNeil.'

'And you are?' Harry said to him.

'I'm DI Inch. This is DS Pirie. We're from Professional Standards.'

They stood looking at each other for a moment, like gunfighters at dawn.

'What can I help you with?' Harry said.

'Grab your coat. You're coming with us to the high street. We can talk there.'

DS Pirie grinned; he was enjoying every moment of this.

Harry grabbed his coat from the incident room. Alex looked at him, puzzled.

The three men walked out.

TWENTY-ONE

'It was fucking awful,' Hector Mann said, pacing about his office, and in that moment, Andrea Mann knew exactly where her son was picking up his bad language from.

'What did they say? And sit down, for God's sake. You'll wear a hole in the carpet.'

'They practically accused me of killing Mhari.'

'What? No. How could they do that?'

'Simple; they get you in an interview room and start accusing you of stuff, hoping for a full confession. They make you feel like crap. I'm surprised they didn't take their batons out and ram them up my arse.'

'Don't be crude.'

He stopped. Gazed out of his office window, looking down into Moray Place. Then he turned back to his wife. 'You don't know what it was like.

You weren't there. They know all about my gambling.'

'So? People are allowed to gamble in this country. It's not communist China.'

'You don't get it; if they think I don't have two pennies to rub together, then they know we can't afford to invest in property. And if they know that, then they know we're all up to something else. Which we are.'

'Jesus, keep your voice down. They don't know shit, that's why they got you in there, to make you sweat like a wee girl. Which you obviously are. They got to you. Sowed the seeds and now you're running about like a chicken who's about to have its body relieved of its head.'

'They keep probing and poking. Especially that daft one from Glasgow. He's unhinged, if you ask me.'

'It's their job to go poking and probing. There was a dead woman in a snowman at the end of our driveway. Did you just expect them to walk away from that?'

'No, but if they keep digging, they'll find something.' Mann turned to look out of the window again.

'Just keep calm,' Andrea said to his back.

There was a knock at the door. 'Not interrupting anything, I hope,' Paul Fox said as he was invited to come in.

'Paul! No, of course not.'

'Hello again, Andrea,' he said, smiling at her.

'Hello, Paul. My husband keeping you busy, then?'

'He certainly is. Plus, the workload from the new St James Centre is keeping us on our toes. But that's what I wanted to talk to you about, Hector. We have another two offers from stores who want a long-term lease. They were just wanting to know certain technical aspects, so I said you could give them a call to discuss. Then I can wrap up the details.'

'That's what I like to hear.' Hector turned to his wife. 'No point in designing a shopping centre that's going to sit empty, is there? Young Paul here is doing sterling work, leasing out the units.'

'Including the hotel at the back that wouldn't look out of place in a sci-fi film?'

'Ah. That's nothing to do with us, thank God,' Hector said to his wife. 'I have to go. Don't go anywhere you don't need to.'

'I have to work too, you know. My business doesn't run itself,' Andrea said.

'Okay, okay.'

'I'll see you in the conference room,' Fox said. 'Good seeing you again, Andrea.'

'You too, Paul.'

They waited until Fox left the room.

'Just be careful. If it doesn't work out now, we'll all end up going to prison,' Mann said.

'You worry too much. Did you hear from Charlie and Lane this morning?'

'No, not yet. I hope to God they call soon.'

'It takes time. Don't rush them, or even worse, panic them. Don't tell them you had to go in to the police station today. You know what a worry wart Charlie is. Big fucking girl that he is.' Mann shook his head in disgust.

They both walked out of Mann's office, then parted, going their own ways.

TWENTY-TWO

'Sorry I'm late,' the man said, walking into the large room. Except it wasn't really a room.

It was a refrigerator.

He smiled at the two people tied to the chairs. 'Cat got your tongue? No?' He laughed as he removed Charlie Henderson's gag. The older man shivered and could hardly talk.

'Your friend hasn't got much to say for herself either.' He grinned and nodded to Lane Mott who sat further away.

Henderson looked at him. Said nothing.

'Did you find what you were looking for?' The man stepped closer. He was wearing a puffer jacket, a hat and gloves. A balaclava covered the lower half of his face. His smile slipped a little bit when Henderson didn't answer.

'I asked you a question, Charlie.'

Henderson tried to talk but couldn't form any words.

'Answer me or I'll take her eyes out.' The man pulled a little ice pick from his pocket.

'N-no. We. D-didn't.'

'Splendid! That's more like it. See what you can achieve when you put your mind to it. But then again, you two would know all about that, wouldn't you?' He turned to Lane. 'Wouldn't you, Lane?'

'How did you know we were here, you fuck?'

The man laughed. 'Hidden cameras, obviously. They alerted me on my phone.'

She looked at him and spat. She obviously had greater resolve than Henderson.

'See? I knew you had the most balls out of all of them. The most fire. I knew it all those years ago. You don't know who I am. Even if I showed my face, you wouldn't know who I was, but that doesn't matter just now. What does matter is you came here, somewhere you don't belong. Just like I knew you would. You didn't fail me.'

'Cowardly bastard,' Lane said, her voice hoarse. She was shivering but she dug deep. 'You're nothing but a fucking coward. Why don't you untie me and when I'm warmed up, you and I can go at it? Fight. Or are you too chicken?' Her eyes were blazing.

He laughed. 'Okay then. You're on!'

He grabbed Henderson's chair, tilted it back and dragged him out of the huge refrigerator. Lane waited and waited, thinking that the man had taken Henderson away to kill him, and then the man was back.

He walked behind her, grabbed her by the hair and tilted her head back. 'I hope you weren't just full of hot air. I'm looking forward to hurting you.' He let her hair go and tilted the chair back.

'Me too, you bastard,' she said, unable to do anything.

There was a bucking motion of the chair as he dragged it out into the old kitchen. Light slanted through the boarded-up windows, and in the corridors where there were no lights on, she could only make out shadows as she was dragged around corners, taken through double doors and then she knew where they were.

The ballroom. He roughly pushed the chair forward so it landed on its four legs and for a second, Lane thought the momentum was going to push her forward so she would fall on her face but it didn't. Her calves were still tied to the chair legs and her feet must have provided enough of a brake to stop her crashing to the floor.

Charlie Henderson was sitting over to one side.

Large curtains had been pulled aside to reveal a wall of windows. The light coming in was almost blinding.

'I'll give you a few moments to let your eyes get adjusted. I wouldn't want you to think this was an unfair fight.'

While they waited, he took his jacket off but kept his balaclava on.

'Why don't you show your face?' Lane said.

'It's surplus to requirements. You don't need to see my face to fight.'

'Coward.'

He strode across to her, moving fast and pulled a knife out of his pocket. Lane gasped for a moment until she felt him behind her, cutting the ropes. He roughly pushed her off the chair, giving himself time to move away from her. He turned briefly and threw the knife at the wall like a knife thrower, where it did nothing more than bounce off and skid across the dance floor.

'Ladies and gentlemen!' he shouted. 'In the red corner, we have reigning champion, the snow killer. In the blue, a new challenger, fighting for her life, Lane Mott!' He clapped loudly. He took his jacket off and laid it on a chair but kept his mask on. Lane struggled to get to her feet, her circulation just starting to return.

He started making motions a boxer might make, punching the air.

The he raised his hands straight up above his head.

'You do understand, Lane, that this is a fight to the death? You kill me, there's a knife there to cut Charlie's ropes. Then you can both leave. That should be a bit of an incentive.'

He walked towards Lane, who was struggling to get up. Or so he thought.

As he got close to her, she suddenly stood up straight and punched him on the nose. As his head was knocked back she went in for an uppercut, but he was too quick for her and dodged it.

He brought his right fist round and it connected with the side of her head, knocking her down.

'What do we have here, ladies and gentlemen?' he shouted, blood starting to run down his face. 'A superb strike by Lane. Was that a lucky shot, or is she one of the best opponents the killer has ever had the good fortune to fight?'

Lane got up and staggered towards him and then she was punching him in a flurry of fists, keeping her head down, and then she was in close, grabbing him. It was exactly like he had told her it was going to be; a fight for her life.

She started pummelling his gut but she could feel the hardness of the muscle there and felt her fear turning to anger. Maybe if she got the better of him, they could get out of this...

The blow hit her hard on the side of the head and

she went sprawling.

'Ladies and gentlemen, the lady with the big mouth just got her arse handed to her on a plate. She—'

Lane launched herself again, this time managing to grab hold of the balaclava and pull it off before the killer could stop her. They both stood still, looking at each other.

Lane looked puzzled. '*You're* doing this. Why?'

He smiled and shrugged. 'Why not?'

'Not good enough.'

'I don't care. It was fucking good enough back then, wasn't it?'

'What are you talking about?' She took a step away from him.

'I think you know what I'm talking about.'

Lane moved fast, swiping the knife up off the floor in one swift movement. 'I'm going to stick you like a pig.'

The killer tracked the movement of the knife with ease as Lane raised it about her head and brought it down. He caught her wrist but didn't bother to try and disarm her. There was no need for that.

He pulled the small ice pick from his trouser pocket and stuck it into Lane's chest. Pulled it out and stabbed her lower down. Then again. Three stab wounds. Three spots of red appearing on her front.

She dropped the knife and fell to the floor.

Charlie Henderson was rocking back and forth in his chair, unable to speak or shout. The shock had gripped hold of him now and his eyes bulged as he took in the scene before him.

The killer wiped the ice pick on Lane's shirt. The wounds were small and hadn't caused a lot of spatter. Not enough to hit the killer.

He walked back to where he had piled his shirt and jacket and quickly got dressed as Lane died from her injuries on the dance floor.

'Come on, Charlie, let's get you back to the fridge.' He grabbed hold of Henderson after closing the huge curtains again. The chair screeched almost as loudly as Henderson as he was dragged back along the corridor, the chair tipped back.

'That's it, Charlie, let it all out. You won't have to wait long until it's your turn. It's going to be all over soon, I promise. I started this little adventure two years ago, but I'm going to finish it soon. Oh, and you might be wondering if they can track your phone. They might look and see where it pinged, but they'll find it was just pinging off the cell tower that deals with Kellerstain. I destroyed it. It's dead, Charlie. Just like you're going to be.'

He put Henderson back in the fridge and closed the door.

Went back for Lane.

TWENTY-THREE

Harry McNeil saw some familiar faces in the high street station. He wasn't allowed to talk to anybody, but having been in Professional Standards himself, he knew the score.

'What am I being investigated for?' he said, sitting down at a table. The two detectives who'd brought him in consulted some notes in front of them.

'I asked you a question,' Harry said, starting to get irritated.

'We'll be right with you,' Pirie said.

'It's sir, when you're addressing me.'

Pirie looked at him. 'I know the rules. Sir.'

'Then abide by them, son. I've been on that side of the table more times than you'll ever dream of. So tell me why I'm here.'

DI Inch looked at him. 'You know better than to try and pull rank in here.'

'You obviously don't listen either, son.'

'You're in here... sir... because a complaint has been lodged against you. A very serious complaint.'

'By whom?'

'We're not at liberty to say.'

'Then tell me what the complaint is, or stop wasting my time.'

'Stalking,' Pirie said. Inch looked at him, like he'd just shown his hand in a game of poker.

'A member of the public has lodged a complaint of stalking and harassment.'

'I deny any knowledge of such incidents. And I have a right to know who's making such statements in order to present a defence. You and I both know that, Inch.'

Inch knew Harry was right. 'A woman who you were involved with, Vanessa Harper, has alleged that you've been standing outside her house watching her, and putting letters through her letterbox in order to scare her.'

Harry made a face. 'What? This is nonsense.'

'You're denying the allegations?' Inch said.

'Of course I am.'

'She alleges you were spying on her on Saturday evening. Standing across the road from her house.'

'What time?'

'Around eight o'clock.'

'Sorry to disappoint you, but I was having a drink with a couple of friends around that time on Saturday night.'

'We'll check up on that. Give us their names.' Inch pushed a pad and pen across to Harry, who wrote down the names Jimmy Dunbar and Dan McLeod, adding their phone numbers.

'She's mistaken. or lying. She's my ex-girlfriend.'

'Rough break up, was it?' Pirie asked.

'None of your business. And since I have a right to have a federation rep with me here, and there isn't one right now, I'll be going. But I will say this before I leave; I am not stalking her.'

'We have the note that was put through her door.'

'Good. Run DNA on it. Check the handwriting sample I'll give you and compare both. You'll see it isn't me.'

'We will. But let me tell you this, DCI McNeil, if we find out that you have been stalking this woman and putting threatening notes through her door, you'll be finished. Your career will be over. Do I make myself understood?'

'I did your job for four years, pal. I know the rules a lot better than you do.' Harry stood up from the table and left the room.

Just outside the front door, he bumped into DI Frank Miller.

'Jesus, Harry, you look frazzled.'

'No wonder. I've just been hauled in to the very department I used to work for.'

'Standards? What did they want with you?'

'Between you and me?'

'Of course.'

'Vanessa, my ex, has reported me for allegedly stalking her. And sending her threatening letters.'

'Jesus, Harry. That's a serious allegation.'

'I know it is. I never thought she would do that to me, Frank. Luckily, I have an alibi for Saturday; I was at home, with Alex. Then I went out to meet a couple of guys, one of whom is also a DCI. The other one is an ex-copper. Maybe you know him; Dan McLeod. Mick Loud, they used to call him.'

'Yeah, I remember him. He and that half-baked brother-in-law of his. Roger Crank. Roger the Dodger they called him. Right nasty bastard. He was on the job, too, until they turfed him out the door.'

'Christ, Crank was McLeod's brother-in-law?'

'Still is, as far as I know.'

'McLeod told me his wife died a few years back. Car accident.'

'Technically, Crank isn't his brother-in-law anymore then. He should steer clear of him.'

'I wonder what Crank's doing now?' Harry said, pulling his collar up against the driving snow.

'I heard he was a taxi driver. He got a plate and owns his own cab.'

'He's better off doing that. At least he isn't taking backhanders. I remember investigating him. Real lowlife.'

'I'm glad I caught you anyway, pal,' Miller said. 'I was going to come round and have a chat with you.'

'About what?'

'The flat. There's no rush, but I'm going to put it up for sale. I thought we could talk about some dates. As I said, no rush though. Kim and I would like to invest the money, that's all...'

'No need to explain, mate. It's your flat. You can sell it any time you want. If you can just give me a wee bit of time to get somewhere else?'

'Jesus, Harry, I said there was no rush and I mean it. You've been a great tenant for years, I'm not expecting you to leave tomorrow.'

'I'll start looking, Frank. I'll call an estate agent and get the ball rolling.'

'Right, buddy, thanks. Now, I better get a move on. I'll be in touch.'

Harry walked up through the vennel and down to Starbucks. He felt like calling Vanessa to find out what the hell she was playing at but he knew that would mean him digging himself a bigger hole. He sent a text to Alex instead.

Bumped into Frank Miller. He's selling the flat. He added a little emoji that was a crying face.

She wrote back a few seconds later. *Oh no! We'll find somewhere just as nice.*

He thought that Alex might think that finding somewhere else was a good thing since Vanessa lived round the corner.

He went on to tell her he would be back down to Fettes shortly.

Then a taxi pulled into the side of the road at Hunter Square and the driver honked the horn. Wound the window down. 'Harry!'

It was Dan McLeod.

'You need a lift?'

Harry was about to go back to the station and get a patrol car to drop him back down the road since Inch had driven him up there, but he opened the taxi door and got in.

'Dan, I was just about to get a patrol to drop me at Fettes.'

'Then it's your lucky day; I'm going home for a bit of lunch. It's on my way.'

'Cheers then, that would be great. I'll get you a pint next time I see you.'

'I'm free tonight, if you like.'

It caught Harry off guard. He had just done telling Alex they would discuss Miller selling the flat and now here was Dan McLeod wanting him to go out again. He didn't want to be one of those boyfriends who had a girlfriend in the house but preferred to spend all his time in the pub.

'I could grab a quick pint.' He didn't want to make a habit of going out with Jimmy Dunbar either and decided he wouldn't mention going out with McLeod again.

'What time? Anytime suits me; I knock off around three.'

'How about eight again?'

'Sure. How about I meet you somewhere?'

'You know Diamonds?'

'Of course. I'm a taxi driver.'

They both laughed as McLeod drove down Cockburn Street.

TWENTY-FOUR

Alex looked worried when Harry got back to Fettes HQ. Dan McLeod had dropped him off at the door.

'Is everything okay?' she asked him.

'Vanessa's made a complaint against me,' he said, after taking her into his office. 'She said I was standing outside her house on Saturday evening, watching her. And leaving threatening notes.' he shook his head.

Alex stood quiet for a moment. 'We know somebody was standing watching her house. I told you, I thought it was you because he was wearing a red jacket like yours.'

'Maybe that's why she thought it was me.'

'Who would be doing this, Harry?'

'I have no idea who would want to scare her. Unless...'

'Unless it's somebody who wants her to *think* it's you.'

'Who would do that?' Then he had the lightbulb moment. 'Ian, your ex.'

Alex didn't know what to say at first. 'You don't think he would do that, do you?'

'You would be in a better position to know that than I would. You used to live with him. Tell me what he was like.'

'He could be hot-tempered at times. Especially after a drink. You just saw a taste of it the other night.'

'Why in God's name would he want to do this? I know young Robbie got in his face, but up to that point, we had never met.'

'He has a jealous streak as well.'

'He's a bloody charmer. I'm going to have a word with him.'

'No, Harry, please don't.'

'I can't let him get away with doing pish like this, Alex.'

'I know.' She was silent for a moment. 'Do what you have to do.'

'Maybe I'll ask Jimmy and Robbie to have a word with him.'

'That might be better.'

Harry's desk phone rang and he answered it. Alex

left his office and a few minutes later, he joined the rest of the team.

'That was Kate Murphy on the phone,' he said. Then to Jimmy Dunbar, 'One of our pathologists. She says that Mhari Baxter had a little fragment in her hair. Ceramic. Like from a tile. As if her head had been bashed against a tiled wall.'

'In somebody's house?' Karen Shiels said.

'Could be. I want you and Simon to go and look around in the Mann's house. Forensics are there today, doing a sweep of their property. Ed Corbett, who owns the place, has given us permission, so we don't need Mann's. I know Mann said he was working today, but if he comes back and gives you any guff, tell him to get raffled.'

'I don't think we'll be hearing from him any time soon,' Alex said.

She couldn't have been more wrong.

Then a phone rang and Eve Bell answered it, holding out the receiver after a few seconds. 'DCI Dunbar? It's for you, sir. One of your team.'

Dunbar got up and took the phone from her. 'Dunbar.' He listened to the caller for a few moments.

'You're sure?' He looked down at the desk for a moment, listening intently.

'Right, thanks.' After he hung up, he looked at Harry. 'I had one of my team go round to Christine

Farr's house and talk to her parents again. It turns out she was through in Edinburgh working. She had been here two days in a row. She got the train back and forth, from Queen Street station.'

'What exactly was she doing here? And how are we just finding that out now?'

'Back then, it was reported by her folks that she went to work as normal. Nothing unusual. We interviewed her boss and co-workers. Christine was working for an engineering company at the time of her death. She was assigned to liaise with a businessman in Glasgow. This man was selling a house and she was responsible for taking notes, photos and the like. But this man had a few properties that he was buying and selling. Christine was out of the office quite a bit.

'In the office, one of Christine's best friends was covering for her. Christine was having an affair with a married man. And that man lived in Edinburgh. Actually he still does. His name is Hector Mann. Christine was getting the train back the night she died, but she had called her friend to tell her she'd missed it and if she didn't get back in to the office next morning, she was going to call in sick.'

'We know she met with the businessman in Glasgow,' Robbie Evans said. 'She left him at lunchtime and his alibi checked out. It was where she went after that, that we drew a blank. Now we know.'

'She was found dead in Glasgow though, wasn't she?' Alex said.

'On the outskirts. Alexandra Park.'

'Bring it up on the screen, Eve,' Harry said. Then to Jimmy, 'Can you show us on the map so we get an idea?'

'Nae bother.' Dunbar walked over to the screen when Eve brought up the map of Glasgow. Dunbar sat beside her and played about with the mouse until he found the park where Christine had been found.

'There.' He pointed to the computer screen, his finger tapping the glass. It showed Alexandra golf course adjoining Alexandra Park.

'Zoom out a bit and put it on satellite view,' Harry said. Dunbar passed the mouse to Eve.

'That park is just off the M8. It's not too far from Glasgow city centre,' Harry said, crouching to look at the screen. He tapped the glass with a pencil.

'Can you identify which part of the park Christine was found?'

'Aye.' He turned to Evans. 'Heid. Point out where in the park Christine was found. I can picture it but I can't see it on here.'

'We'll never have to worry about the old 'uns taking over the world, eh? The technology would blow their brains out.'

'Shut your pie hole and start working that mouse.'

Dunbar budged his chair over so Evans could bring his in. He took over the mouse and zoomed in. 'She was found just inside the gate. The vehicle gates were locked, but if you look at the street view, you'll see there's a pedestrian entrance next to it that's open. Opposite, on the other side of the road, an old, little dead-end street. They blocked it off years ago. It crosses over the old railway line that they made into a walkway.'

'And that's where you think he parked?' Harry said.

'Aye. We figured he had her in a car, and parked it there. Cars park there all the time, so it wouldn't stick out. So, let's say, he takes her out the car and somebody comes, he leaves himself the option of just dumping her over the iron wall, which is around waist level or so. But even though the main road runs past there, and he would have to cross four lanes to get to the pedestrian entrance, it's still quiet at night.'

Dunbar looked away from the screen. 'It would only take him four seconds to cross that road at three o'clock in the morning. We know, we reconstructed it. One of the boys had a WPC over his shoulder and he waited until there was no traffic coming. He ran over, got inside the park and hid with her in under ten seconds.'

'Let's assume she was indeed over here in Edinburgh and he picked her up, we reckon he kept her from the last time she was seen in the offices, until she was discovered. And her tissue suggested she had been frozen, according to the post-mortem report. Look at that though.'

Harry pointed to the screen. 'It had been snowing heavily the last day she was seen. I'm thinking he wouldn't have risked killing her and then transporting her from Edinburgh to Glasgow. What was the weather report like for the days leading up to when she was found?'

Dunbar opened the manila folder that was on the desk in front of him and leafed through some papers. 'It was cold but dry. No more snow for another week.'

'That means the gritters would have been out and it would have been easy for him to drive through on the M8, dump her and then drive back. Look at the map; if he came down that little road, Dee Street, he could have connected with Cumbernauld Road, hooked a right and gone back up Provan Road, past the gate to the park where he'd just dumped her, and a few minutes later, back on the M8 heading back to Edinburgh.'

Dunbar moved his chair back. 'All this time, we've been looking for some Glasgow psycho, and the bastard's been here in Edinburgh.'

TWENTY-FIVE

It was late afternoon when Harry and Dunbar were finally able to track Hector Mann down. He had finished early for the day and was doing some work in his home office. His wife was there, trying to shepherd the kids to their little table where they could sit out of the way without disturbing the detectives.

'Come through to my office,' Mann said, leading them across the hall to a room with two French doors. It looked exactly like what a home office should look like; a desk, chair, computer, some filing cabinets and a small couch for skiving. A small TV sat on a cabinet.

'My apologies about the way I acted in the interview. I'm still in shock about Mhari. God, what a day. Run off my bloody feet and then I come home and I still have more work to do. My wife thinks I have it easy, like I'm in here watching Netflix. Chance would be a fine thing. You want a coffee?' he asked, pointing to his Keurig machine that sat along from the TV.

'No thanks,' Harry said. Dunbar also declined.

Mann sat down behind his desk, inviting the detectives to sit on the small couch. Harry wondered if the little boy was allowed in here to jump up and down on this one.

'Have you found out any more about Mhari's killer?'

'Not exactly. We wanted to ask about your affair with Christine Farr,' Harry said.

Mann shot forward, looking through the glass panes of the doors. 'What makes you ask that? Why would you think I was having an affair with her? How dare you! Get out.'

'Get a hold of yourself,' Dunbar said. 'Or would you like us to ask your wife in here too, to ask her?'

The fight left Mann and he sat back. 'For God's sake, my wife can't find out.'

'Trust me, if we find out you killed her, the whole of the UK will know you were having an affair. Your wife will be the last person you'll have to worry about. The next person you'll be having an affair with might have a beard and belly hair.'

'God Almighty. I swear I didn't kill her.'

'Tell us about that day. The day she was last seen,' Harry said.

Mann drummed his fingers on the edge of his desk, as if deciding what the lesser of two evils was; his wife mutilating his manhood, or a man with rougher hands doing it in prison.

'She was coming through from Glasgow, to see me. Her friend knew about us, but not her family, apparently. She had told her folks that she was coming through on a job.'

'Was your wife ever suspicious?' Dunbar asked.

'No, never. I deal with a lot of people in my job, men and women. Christine was just another woman I was dealing with.'

'We'd like you to give us a DNA sample,' Harry said, bringing an envelope out of his pocket. Inside was a swab inside a tube.

'Okay. Anything you want. I didn't kill Christine. I told police that at the time. We were all questioned because she was in the office, but I'll do whatever you want.'

Harry put on a glove and handed the swab to Mann, who then put it in his mouth and swabbed the inside of his cheek. He handed it back and the swab was put in the tube and the evidence bag sealed.

'How was your relationship with Christine?' Dunbar asked.

'We got on very well. She was fun to be around, we

had a good laugh and we went for a few drinks then we would... you know...'

'Where did you have sex?' Dunbar asked bluntly.

'Here. When I knew Andrea was going to be working late with a client.'

'And she never suspected a thing?'

Mann shook his head. 'Listen, I love my wife, but sometimes she's just a bit... mental. She has a temper on her.'

'And you're sure she never found out about Christine?' Harry said.

'And killed her, you mean? No. I think she would have killed me before she killed Christine.'

'Okay, Mr Mann, we'll have this DNA run through the system. It won't be overnight, but we will get a result.' The two policemen left the house and Andrea Mann came in.

'What now?' she said.

'They think I was having an affair with Christine. I had to tell them I was. For everybody's sake.'

'You did well. That should keep them off our backs for a while.'

TWENTY-SIX

'I haven't been here in years,' Alex said to Robbie Evans as she pulled her car into the little car park outside the Centurion pub. It sat on the corner of Featherhall Avenue. Next to it was a bookies and a hairdressing supply shop.

'You could buy your hair dye here, lose your money on a horse then go into the pub to drink your sorrows away,' Evans said. 'I like this place.'

'I don't dye my hair, I don't gamble and it's too early for getting blootered,' Alex said, as they got out into the cold.

'The printer's it is, then.'

They headed onto the main road. It was a busy thoroughfare, the main road leading to Glasgow back in the days before the motorway opened up.

'I want to thank you for helping me at the flat the other night,' Alex said. 'Ian has a bit of a temper.'

'You could have handled yourself with him, no doubt. But I'm always on hand to help out a colleague.'

'You're not as bad as DCI Dunbar makes you out to be.'

'Why? What has the old sod been saying now?'

Alex laughed. 'Nothing. But I want to buy you both a meal before you head back.'

'God knows when that will be, Alex. We pretty much have free rein. If we go back with our tails between our legs, then words will be said by the chief super.'

'At least you're in a nice wee hotel, with all your needs taken care of.'

'True. And I don't have to share a room with the boss. I don't have to look at him walking about in his vest and skids. That would give me the fear.' They walked along St John's Road, past the bank on the opposite corner to the pub. 'How long have you and Harry been dating?'

Alex stopped so suddenly that Evans thought there was something wrong with her. 'Did he tell you?'

'What? No. I just assumed. What with the way you both look at each other.'

'It's that obvious?'

'Of course it is.'

'Jesus, I didn't think it showed that much.' They started walking again.

'A blind man can see it.'

'Damn it. We've just started dating, and we don't want anybody to know yet.'

'You're secret's safe with me.' He grinned at her. They walked forward and came to the little printer's shop.

They stepped out of the snow and into the warmth. There was a counter facing them with a young woman standing behind it.

'Hi. How can I help?' she asked with a smile.

They showed their warrant cards. 'We wanted to ask you about a card that was printed here. A Christmas card.'

'Last year?' the woman asked.

'Not sure to be honest. I have a photograph of it on my phone if you could take a look. It has your company name on the back.'

Alex fished her iPhone out and opened up the photo app. 'This is it here.'

The woman took the phone from her and had a closer look. The snow-covered tree, with the Christmas lights on. The snowman standing next to it.

'Were there no names inside? Like, Merry Christmas from the Smiths, something like that?'

'Nothing. I assumed it was usual to put a family or company name inside.'

'It is. Normally people would do that, but there have been people who just want a photo made into a card with nothing inside so they can write a personal message. We always print our company name on the back.'

'Yes,' Evans said. 'I don't suppose you recognise it?'

'No, it doesn't jump out. Let me ask my dad. He's through the back. It's his business and he's worked here since before Noah built the Ark.'

'I heard that, young lady,' an old man said, coming through the beaded curtains from the back. They could hear a printer working away through the back.

'They want to know if you recognise this,' she said, showing the older man the photo on the phone.

'Yes, I do.' He handed the phone back. 'It's from Norwood House, the hotel along the road past Ingliston.'

'The hotel would have had this made up then?' Alex asked.

'No. They had similar ones made up, with a Christmas message and their name on the front. The tree would be in front of the door. Well, it was on the other side of the small car park entrance, but the way it was taken, it looked like it was right at the entrance.

My wife and I used to go there for a meal. I remember it well.'

'Why was this one taken?'

'A young man brought the photo in. Said he wanted some cards printed up for the people in the hotel to send out to friends.'

'Did he give his name?'

'Yes, but I don't have a record of it. I remember he paid cash.'

'You don't have copies of a receipt?' Evans asked.

'Not from back then. It must have been about ten years ago now. Something like that, I don't remember exactly when.'

'Really?' Alex said. 'How come you remember him and he paid cash?'

The man smiled. 'He was a nice boy. It was a surprise for his mum. He told me he was the one who built the snowman. The manager at the time loved it. The boy was really pleased.'

'No idea of his name?' Evans said.

'No. I didn't see him much after that. I never met his mother, but I believed she worked there. It's closed down, more's the pity.'

'How long has it been closed?'

'Oh, let me see.' He stared off into space for a moment. 'I took your mother there for her sixtieth and that was the last time we were there, so that would be, over two years ago now. Terrible shame. It's up for sale, but nobody seems to be interested.'

'Thanks for your help,' Alex said.

'Any time. And if you need anything printed, like wedding invitations or something, give us a call and I'll give you a discount.'

Alex could feel her cheeks going red and just smiled before they left the shop.

'It seems that everybody knows about me and Harry.'

Evans laughed. 'You're paranoid. Nobody knows and it will stay that way until you tell them.'

'It's not true what Jimmy says about you.'

TWENTY-SEVEN

'Penny for them,' Harry said, coming into the living room. He had just finished putting the dishes into the dishwasher.

'What? Oh, I was just thinking about why Mhari Baxter would have that old Christmas card in her belongings.'

'And what was her connection to the old hotel?' He sat down beside her.

'By the way, Robbie Evans knows about us.'

'He does? How?'

'He guessed. Honestly, talk about wearing your heart on your sleeve. He already thought we were going out. Apparently, I look at you funny.'

'Funny?'

'Not funny, but with a doe-eyed look, like I'm madly in love with you.'

'But you are.'

She smiled at him. 'Yes, I am, but other people could see it.'

'He's keeping it to himself though, isn't he?'

'Yes. We'll have a big announcement one day, but until then, it will be our dirty little secret.' She leaned over and kissed him. He held onto her until she gently pushed him away.

'You're going for a pint with Dan McLeod, remember?'

'Oh, yeah. I can't be bothered to be honest but I think he's lonely.'

'If he doesn't have anybody at home, then he's bound to be.'

Harry stood up. 'I'm going to jump in the shower and get ready.'

'Don't mind me. I'm going to have a relaxing night in front of the TV. As well as looking for other houses on my iPad.'

Half an hour later, Harry was ready and put his jacket on.

'Why don't I drive you there?' Alex said.

'No, don't be daft. It's not far.'

'It's uphill. In the snow.'

'It's no worse than what my parents had to endure when they were walking to school.'

She laughed. 'Call me if you want me to pick you up.'

'That would be spoiling me. But I'd rather you be safe here.'

'I could get used to this, somebody caring about me.'

'I'll let you get the kettle on when I get home. I don't want to be out too late.'

He left after grabbing his red jacket. He wanted to be seen at night, unlike some of the people he saw walking about with black clothing on in the dark. It was even worse when it was raining. Organ donors, Harry called them.

Outside, the snow had stopped for the time being. A gritter truck passed him by, going up the hill. He took it easy, walking carefully, and made it up to the top, and then it was down Dean Park Crescent and into Dean Street where Diamonds bar was located.

He took a deep breath before going in.

Here we go, he thought, pushing the door open.

TWENTY-EIGHT

'*Lethal Weapon*,' Robbie Evans said. They'd moved on from who was the hardest actor to what the best movies ever made were.

'What? *Lethal Weapon*? Pish. *To Kill A Mockingbird*, now that's a classic movie.'

'I've never seen it.'

'Why doesn't that surprise me?' The windscreen wipers were on intermittent, wiping the snow away from the glass.

'Another one; *Jaws*.'

Dunbar looked at his young sergeant. 'Now you're talking. I agree with that one. I loved that film. *You're going to need a bigger Land Rover*,' he said, paraphrasing the line from the movie.

'*One Flew Over the Cuckoo's Nest*.'

'Christ, Robbie, you're on fire tonight.'

'I know. I have a side to me that nobody knows about.'

'The one where you dress up in your mother's clothes?'

'That's not very nice, boss.' He looked through the windscreen and pointed. 'Isn't that him there?'

Dunbar looked closer. 'It is indeed. Big wanker.'

Ian Wallace had come out of his communal stair in the tenement building and put a bag of rubbish in the black communal bin that sat by the side of the road.

They were in the marked car and Wallace looked across at them, turning to go back in his stair, when he thought better of it, turned back and strode across to their big car.

Dunbar wound the window down as Wallace came up.

'Have you two got nothing better to do than sit about outside my flat?'

'We lead boring lives, what can I tell you?'

'This is fucking harassment.'

'No it's not. We're waiting for a friend.'

'Tell McNeil he's a twat and he'd better not start with me. Or else.'

'That a threat, laddie?'

'My lawyer will deal with him. Pass that on.'

'You need to walk away, son. Next time somebody

comes to have a word, they might no' be as friendly as us.'

'Now who's threatening?'

'Walk away. Let it go. I'm not in the habit of telling somebody twice.' The older Glaswegian detective made eye contact with Wallace and the ex-firefighter seemed to get the message. He said nothing more as he shivered and walked away into his flat.

'*Little Women*,' Evans said as he pulled the big car away.

'What?'

'*Little Women*. That was a great film.'

'I think you're just taking the piss now.'

'I'm not, boss, honestly. And *Wuthering Heights*.'

'Stop talking.' Just then, Dunbar got the text he'd been waiting for. 'Right. Get a move on, son. You know where we're going.'

TWENTY-NINE

Dan McLeod was sitting at a table and got up to get Harry a drink when he saw him come in.

'Cheers, Dan.'

'Here's tae us, my old friend.'

'I thought you worked the night shift, Dan?' Harry said. The place was busy, with a few men standing in groups and a couple of women sitting at a table.

'I do mostly day shifts but I work the nights Friday and Saturday.'

'That's where the money is, right enough,' Harry said.

'Your pals not coming along tonight? Jimmy Dunbar and young Robbie.'

'No, they're having a conference call with their colleagues in Glasgow.'

'Fair enough.'

They talked about the old days and had a laugh for a while, then Harry got another round in.

McLeod drank some of his pint then looked at Harry. 'I wanted to run something by you, mate, and although I hadn't seen you for ages, I wanted an opinion.'

'Okay. Fire away.'

'I met a woman. Actually, she was a passenger, and we hit it off right away. I asked her out for a drink, and she said yes, but now I'm having second thoughts.'

'Why?'

'Margo, that's why. I feel like I'm cheating on her, Harry.'

'Don't be daft. I mean, I've never lost a wife like you have, but there comes a time when you have to move forward. It doesn't mean to say you're robbing yourself of the memory of Margo, but life can get lonely.'

'You got divorced, didn't you?'

'I did. Things just didn't work out for us and we went our separate ways. No harm, no foul. I can't imagine losing my wife, like you.'

'It was hard.' McLeod took a sip of his pint and set the glass down on the table. 'I told her not to drive that night, but she wouldn't listen. She was going too fast for the conditions, they said. It was raining heavily.

They reckon she lost control of the car and it hit the overpass doing seventy-five. She was killed instantly.'

Harry took a sip of his own lager. 'Jesus, I'm sorry, Dan. That must have been so hard.'

'It was. I felt like taking my own life. I started drinking too much. I couldn't get out of bed in the morning. That's why I wanted to get out of the job. And it worked. I felt better as time went on, but now I've met this woman and I don't know if I want to go out with her or not.'

'Nobody can make that decision for you, Dan, but if you do go out and you find it's not for you, then you've lost nothing.'

'That's true.' He laughed. 'Look at us; older blokes with girlfriends. You'll have to introduce me to yours. Maybe we could do a foursome some night.'

Harry wasn't sure if he meant Vanessa or Alex, but then he realised it had to be Vanessa, because McLeod wouldn't know about Alex.

'We'll see, Dan. The thing is, Vanessa and I split up.'

'Oh God, I'm sorry. There I go, putting my big foot in it again.'

'Don't worry about it.' Just then, Harry's phone dinged with a text message. He took his phone out and looked at it. It was from Vanessa.

Why are you outside my house again? Leave me alone!

He thought about it for a moment, on the fence about whether he should reply or not. 'Talk of the devil.'

He sent a text back. *What are you talking about. I'm in the pub with a friend.*

I'm going to call the police if you don't go away.

I'm not there, Vanessa.

If it's not you, then who is it?

Maybe it's better if you do call the police. They'll see it's not me.

If you come round and the guy's still outside, then I'll believe it with my own eyes. Come round now, Harry. Prove to me it's not you and I promise I'll leave you alone.

Harry tutted.

'Anything wrong, pal?' Dan said.

'I need to go, Dan. Sorry. Something's come up.'

'Ach, nae bother. It was good seeing you for a wee while. We can do it again, yes?'

'Of course. I'll give you a call.'

Harry stepped out into the cold night air, knowing now that Vanessa wasn't playing games.

The two women from the bar came out behind him as he stepped over the road to the waiting Audi and got in the back seat next to Jimmy Dunbar.

'*A Christmas Carol* or *It's a Wonderful Life?*' Dunbar asked. Robbie Evans was sitting up front, while Alex was behind the wheel of her car.

'The George C. Scott version or The Muppets?'

'Scott.'

'Definitely *Wonderful Life*'

'See?' he said turning to Evans.

'Well, I prefer the Muppet one.'

'That's because you're a Muppet.'

'You sure he won't see me?' Harry asked, looking through the side window but shrinking down a bit.

'They're tinted. He won't see in,' Alex said.

'And the patrol Land Rover is parked away from our flat?'

'Relax, Harry, this is not our first rodeo,' Dunbar said.

'Sorry, but this has got me on edge.'

They watched as Dan McLeod walked down the road a bit and got in behind the wheel of his taxi. The diesel engine clattered into life.

'I thought he was getting the bus?' Dunbar said.

'He said he was.' Harry watched as the taxi drove by and connected with Dean Park Crescent and drove up the hill. 'He probably forgot to tell me he was going to be drinking and driving.'

The taxi disappeared out of sight.

THIRTY

The big man was staggering down the hill, trying not to slip on the icy pavement. He was leaning on a snow-topped hedge, trying to light a cigarette when the taxi pulled in. The driver jumped out and made his way carefully round the front.

'Got a light, mate?' the big man said, pushing off the hedge and blocking his way.

'No, I don't smoke.'

'Aw, come on, man, give's a fucking light,' he slurred.

'Look, get out of my way,' Dan McLeod said.

The front door to the house behind the drunk man opened.

'What's going on?' a voice said.

'This arsehole wants a light and won't get out the way. I don't want to cause a fuss.'

The drunk turned round and started walking up the path. 'You got a light, mate?'

'Naw. Now piss off,' said the man at the door.

'Aw, come on. How about a wee swally?' The drunk staggered up to the doorstep and tripped, pushing the homeowner backwards and landing on top of him.

'Help me, for fuck's sake,' the guy said, pinned under the big drunk, who was wrestling.

McLeod shot forward and tried to haul the drunk of the man pinned beneath him.

None of them saw the red car pull in behind the taxi. Or the other car following it.

'What's happening here?' Robbie Evans shouted.

Dan McLeod turned round to look at him. 'None of your business, pal. Piss off.'

The drunk was on his knees and got up, pushing past the man on the floor. Harry had been right; sure enough it was Roger Crank. McLeod tried to grab him but he was in the house now. Crank got up and charged at the drunk.

The big drunk, DC Simon Gregg, turned round and easily deflected the punch, grabbing Crank's arm and twisting it up his back.

'I used to be a fucking copper,' Roger Crank said. 'I'll have somebody kick your fucking head in.'

McLeod rushed Gregg as well but Evans put his

foot out and tripped him up. 'I'm a police officer. And so is he. And the bloke behind me. Oh, and you know Harry McNeil. We're all fucking coppers.'

Alex, and the females from the pub, Eve Bell and Karen Shiels, all crowded into the hallway.

'Let us get by, sir,' Alex said, rushing past and into Vanessa's living room.

They found her tied to a chair, a gag in her mouth.

'Harry, what's going on?' McLeod said. 'I just got a call to come here and...'

'Stop talking pish, Dan. It's over.'

McLeod let out a roar and ran at Harry but Evans stepped forward and headbutted McLeod. 'Oops, he ran into me.'

McLeod fell in a heap. Crank was struggling, but Gregg had a tight hold of him. Eve Bell stepped forward and handcuffed him. Harry walked past and into the living room where Alex and Karen were untying Vanessa.

'Jesus, Van, you okay?'

She was crying. 'He took my phone, Harry. He said you were going to get the blame for this. I think they were going to kill me.'

Two figures appeared in the doorway, making their way past the struggling men in the hallway.

'Do you mind telling those officers there what you just told me?' Harry said.

DI Inch and DS Pirie from Standards looked at Vanessa. 'I'm sorry, I got it wrong. It wasn't Harry at all. It was that monster in the hall.'

'Roger Crank?' Inch asked.

'I don't know his name. He took my phone and I saw him texting on it. I don't know what it said.'

Harry showed Inch the text message Crank had sent him.

'We'll get them up the station and charged. I'll assign other detectives to deal with this, but we'll need your statements.'

'No problem. And thanks for your cooperation, DI Inch.'

'We only want to get to the truth.' They walked out of the room and Harry excused himself. Looked at McLeod who was being restrained.

'Why, Dan?'

McLeod looked at him. 'When you were investigating Roger, my Margo was beside herself. He was her brother. The night she died, she was on her way to see him, but she was so upset, she lost control of her car. All because of you! We've been planning this for a long time. When I saw you the other night, I was sitting at the side of the road, waiting for you to come out. How did you figure out we were setting you up?'

'Something somebody said to me, reminding me you were Crank's brother-in-law.'

'I hope you rot in hell, McNeil.'

'You first.'

The two men were hauled out of the house. Harry went back in to see Vanessa, who was now untied.

'I was stupid, Harry. But I realise what I lost.'

Alex excused herself and left the room. The others did too, leaving only Harry and Vanessa.

'It's life, Ness. Things happen.'

'I was stupid. Playing stupid games to try and get you back. But I realise you've moved on now.'

He stood looking at her for a moment. 'I have.'

Vanessa looked away for a moment. 'I've decided to sell the business, and this house too. I'm moving out of the area.'

'You don't have to do that on my account.'

'I'm not. I'm doing it for me. And I'm sorry for what I put you through.'

When he got outside, his team were dealing with McLeod and Crank. Dunbar and Evans, were standing off to the side. Uniformed patrols had also turned up.

'What a bloody night, but thanks for helping me out,' Harry said to Dunbar. 'I just had to be sure it wasn't Ian Wallace. And when Alex said she saw a guy with a red jacket on standing out here when I was meeting you and McLeod for a drink, I wondered who it could be. Then Frank Miller mentioned Crank owned a taxi, and with McLeod being his brother-in-law, it got me wondering.'

'That's what we're here for, pal.' Dunbar walked over to the front door on the passenger side of the black cab, where a driver would keep his personal belongings as there was no front seat. He pulled open the door and they all saw a red jacket that was similar to Harry's, and could easily be mistaken for his at a distance.

'I reckon he wanted to get you out of the house, so it would look like you were pestering Vanessa.'

'If it wasn't for you lot helping me out, I might have gone down for this.'

'Just make sure me and the boy here get an invite to your wedding.' He nodded at Alex. Who just grinned back.

'See you in the morning, Jimmy. We still have a killer to catch.'

'Do you think everybody knows?' Harry said as Alex came through with two coffees.

'Apparently. Robbie said he could see the way we looked at each other.'

'I can understand you, ogling a God like me...'

Alex put a hand up. 'Give up while the going's good.'

He laughed. 'You're right. I'll just shut up now.'

'I was thinking about things earlier,' she said. 'First, let me ask you; do you like living in this flat?'

'Of course I do. It's the reason Vanessa and I split up, remember? She wanted me to give the place up and I wouldn't.'

'Hear me out then; why don't you and I buy this place?'

He sat silently for a moment. 'I never thought about that.'

'I get half the proceeds from my flat, and we could get a mortgage for whatever we need to finance.'

He nodded and drank some of his coffee. 'Before my ex moved to Fife, she bought me out. I invested the money. I could put that down on this place and we could mortgage whatever was left.'

'If you don't think we're rushing things.'

'No, it sounds fine to me. We could get a lawyer to draft things up. If you have more money than me to put in, then if anything went pear-shaped further down the line, we would each get back what we put in and...'

She smiled and put a finger on his lips. 'We're going to make this work, Harry. I'm a very loyal and devoted woman. Ian knew that, and you're going to find that out. We'll make it. I have no doubts.'

'I'll call Frank Miller in the morning.'

'First though...' She stood up and took him by the hand.

He didn't fight it.

THIRTY-ONE

'I spoke to that DI Inch this morning,' Dunbar said. 'At first, he wasn't going to tell me anything, but I reminded him that he was completely on the wrong track accusing you and that would go on his record. I also told him I would be writing a report, and I could include him in a good light or a bad light, and that shut his pie hole for him. He then told me they're going to throw the book at that pair of bastards. Kidnapping, assault, all sorts of stuff.'

'I appreciate that,' Harry said.

'Nae bother, pal. We all did a good job last night, even you, Robbie.'

'Backhanded compliment, that was,' Evans said, as he steered the car along the A90, past Ingliston.

'Better than a poke in the eye with a sharp stick.'

'Here it is, up here on the left,' Alex said, leaning forward and pointing.

Evans brought the car down to a slower speed before getting into the left-hand lane and turning into the hotel driveway. There were some tracks, but mostly covered up by fresh snow. It was uphill and zig-zagged but the big, heavy car took care of it.

The went under a low, narrow bridge that carried the Edinburgh to Glasgow railway line. At the top, the hotel came into view.

'It was a big house, many moons ago, belonging to a brewing family,' Alex said.

Dunbar looked at her.

'I did some homework last night.'

'You should read sometimes,' he said, turning to Evans. 'You might learn something.'

'I do read.'

'The *Beano* doesn't count.'

The old building was boarded up but was still in good condition. Harry looked at the For Sale sign near the entrance. The listing company was Crawford and partners. The agent to contact was Paul Fox.

Evans was about to drive forward when Harry put a hand on his shoulder. 'Stop right there.'

He opened the back door and they all got out.

'What do you see?' Dunbar asked.

'There. That tree. Come this way.' He had already

sent them the photo of the Christmas card that Mhari Baxter had had in her possession. He walked round the tree until they were facing the hotel. Took his phone out and looked at the card.

'This is it. The view of the hotel, just like that printer told you yesterday.'

They all looked at it and agreed it was.

'Just imagine it with a snowman and coloured lights round the tree and there you have it.'

'What was Mhari doing with it?' Harry said.

'The old man in the printer's said that it wasn't the hotel that had it made up as they had their own. This was a personal photo that somebody had made into a card.'

'And the only person that can tell us who, is dead,' Dunbar said.

'I wonder where those tracks came from?' Evans said.

'It's for sale, so maybe somebody came to look at it,' Harry said. 'Alex can you call that number on the For Sale sign and ask that Fox guy?'

'No problem.' She walked away and took her phone out. They could hear her calling somebody and they started walking round the building. They came to a set of glass doors, making up part of a wall. Harry went over and put his hands up to the glass to look inside.

He pulled on a pair of gloves and tried one of the door handles but it was locked.

'Anything?' Jimmy Dunbar said.

'It looks like a ballroom. There's a couple of chairs sitting in the middle of the floor. Nothing unusual.'

They were about to walk away when Harry spotted something outside one of the other doors. A few drops of blood, not covered by any snow.

'Jimmy. Look down there.'

Alex came back round the corner and looked. 'Paul Fox said the hotel has been for sale for over two years. It was owned by the Norwood family for a long time but after the owner died, none of the family members wanted to run it. It eventually closed.' She looked down at the dark spots on the concrete.

'Blood?' she said.

'Could be,' Dunbar said. There were handles on the other doors. Dunbar pulled on a pair of gloves and tried one. The door opened.

They stepped out of the cold and into the warmth of the hotel. It was obvious the heating was still on.

They were on the stage at the far end of the ballroom where wedding receptions had been held. At either end was a small staircase leading down to the dance floor.

They went down. Light was coming in through the large windows but there were still shadows. They approached the chairs sitting in the middle of the ballroom floor, where perhaps there'd been the celebration of two people getting married, or maybe parties celebrating the anniversary of a couple's nuptials.

There was a dark red stain round one of the chairs.

'You think Mhari was here?' Alex said. 'Maybe where she was killed?'

'Could be. She knew something about this hotel and for some reason came back here?' Harry looked around. 'The medical report said she was frozen before she was kept out in the snow. Let's see if we can find a freezer.'

The four of them filed out of the ballroom. Harry turned to Alex. 'Call it in. I want forensics out here. And can you call Paul Fox back and ask when was the last time somebody had a look round here. Like a prospective buyer.'

She took her phone out and called Fox back but the call broke up. 'I'll take this outside,' she said, going back into the ballroom and up and out through the back doors. Harry, Dunbar and Evans were standing in a corridor that was dimly lit.

'Wouldn't it make sense if that was where the meals were served for a wedding reception, that the kitchen would be close by?' Evans said. 'I mean, the big kitchen would have a big fridge and freezers, I assume.'

Dunbar looked at him. 'We'll make a detective out of you yet. Lead the way.'

They went back into the ballroom and saw swing doors at the back. They went through, and Harry took his phone out and switched the LED light on. It was indeed the kitchen area. It was large, with all the usual worktops, ovens and utensils that belonged in an industrial kitchen.

'There are more doors over there,' Harry said. They walked over and opened one of them, discovering it led into a huge dining room for guests at the hotel. Moving back into the kitchen, they saw large doors against one wall. Harry opened one of the doors and shone his light inside.

There was row upon row of stainless steel shelving with no food on them. A walk-in freezer door was open.

'This could have been the place,' Dunbar said. Then he turned to Evans. 'Stay outside the door. This isn't some cheap horror film where everybody gets trapped in a big fridge by the killer.'

'I'll give you a shout if I see some bam with a big knife.'

'I suppose he could have locked the door from the outside, or blocked it somehow. That would explain why Mhari's body was deep frozen,' Harry said.

'We still don't know why,' Dunbar said.

'I think the rest of them know why but they're sticking together. Maybe it's time to give them another roasting.'

They left the refrigerated room.

'Go and see if Alex has made contact with the estate agent again,' Dunbar said to Evans.

THIRTY-TWO

This would have been a nice place to have a wedding reception, Alex thought as she walked into the middle of the little car park. At the far end, there was another narrow road leading off. She walked across it as she dialled Paul Fox's number again.

She knew she was getting ahead of herself, with all the thoughts of a wedding, but she'd known Harry about eight months, and although it had been strictly professional up to this point, she felt she knew him a lot better than she had ever known Ian Wallace. Her ex-fiancé had been standoffish at times.

Maybe by the time she and Harry decided if they wanted to spend the rest of their lives together, this place would be under new management.

But would she want to have her wedding reception in a place where there had been a possible murder?

Probably not.

Fox's phone rang and then went to voicemail. Crap. She kept walking, following the tracks of the vehicle that had been here recently. Maybe a romantic couple had come here for a bit of privacy in their back seat.

Or maybe it was just Paul Fox showing somebody around the property. That would make more sense.

The little road led through to some buildings. She saw them through the snow-covered trees. Then she saw something else. Or was it her imagination?

Somebody had been standing watching her. She moved to get a better look but couldn't see anybody. She started walking forward. She tried Paul Fox again. Nothing. Then she caught movement in her peripheral vision. Could it be a deer up here? Was it a branch being moved by the wind?

There was a house on her left, and one straight ahead, standing sideways to her. Across from that was another house but facing her straight on was a garage block.

She stood listening; she could hear the distant rumble of traffic. The M8 and M9 converged at Newbridge so there was plenty of traffic going about. She walked forward, looking at the house on her left. It seemed still, with nothing having disturbed the snow around it.

The movement had come from near the garage block, she was sure.

She could call Harry, but if it was just her overactive imagination, then he wouldn't be too pleased. No, she was a big girl. She could deal with this on her own.

She approached the garage block. The snow had stopped now but what had come down overnight had made the place look like no one had walked here in years.

The tracks she had been following had disappeared. Surely if somebody were here, then there would have been car tracks?

She smiled. It was just her imagination at work. She reached the garage doors and pulled at one. They opened easily as if somebody had recently cleared the snow from in front of them. As the shaft of light shone inside, she heard the crunch of snow behind her, and turned, thinking it was Robbie Evans, sent to get her.

It wasn't Evans.

The man wore all black, including the mask that covered his face, leaving only his eyes visible. He launched himself at her, sending her flying but she managed to grab the edge of the door to stop herself falling. Her left fist tried to strike the man's face but he easily deflected it. She straightened up, blocking a punch with one hand while she tried to look at her phone with the other. He knocked it from her grasp.

Alex knew how to fight. Her dad had instilled that in her for the longest time. Hit them with anything you have. That was before her police training, but she knew this guy was powerful and strong.

She had one weapon in her arsenal that she hadn't used in a long time.

She screamed.

It had no immediate effect on her attacker, then he suddenly stopped and pushed her roughly to the ground. He ran into the garage and then she heard a car start up. She sat up and then rolled to one side as the car shot out of the garage and made for the exit.

Then she saw Robbie Evans running towards her. That's why the attacker had left her.

'Jesus, Alex, are you okay?' he said, racing up to her.

'I'm fine. Thank God you were coming.'

'I heard the scream.' He got her to her feet. 'Are you hurt?'

'No, just my pride.'

'Did you get a look at him?'

'No, but I saw the car and I got the plate number.'

'Thank God. Come on, let's get you back to the hotel.'

Harry and Dunbar were outside when they saw Alex and Evans rushing towards them.

'She was attacked!' Evans shouted. 'I've called it in.'

'Christ, are you alright?' Harry said, rushing to Alex.

'Yes, I'm fine. But Robbie saved my life. I think the guy would have killed me.' She told them about her assailant and the car.

'What did the PNC come back with?' Harry asked Evans.

'Registered to a male owner. One Charlie Henderson.'

THIRTY-THREE

'He's probably just nipped down to the M8 from the Norwood House hotel,' Alex said. 'He left by the back road and it's only a couple of minutes to the motorway.'

'That would be too easy,' Harry said. 'I want to go and speak to the Corbetts again, the people who own Kellerstain.'

Patrol cars arrived, followed by the forensics team. Harry told Maggie Parks what they were looking at and where her and her team should start. He also wanted uniforms to search the whole hotel.

'And find that Paul Fox. I want a complete rundown on this hotel.'

'I think we should go and talk to Hector Mann,' Dunbar said, 'since we're going to Kellerstain anyway.'

In the Land Rover, they took the main road down to Newbridge, then along the A8 then cut through the bank's world headquarters, which had a little exit on Gogar Station Road, then they turned into Kellerstain.

Alex was on her phone while Evans was driving. 'Mann's wife is at home, but Mann himself is out on a job. She can't get hold of him.'

'We'll talk to her after the Corbetts. Make sure uniform don't let her go anywhere. Arrest her if they have to.'

'I warned them about Henderson and his car.'

Ed Corbett and his wife were visibly shaken when they arrived. Amber Dodds and Rose Ashland were sitting in the conservatory with a uniformed officer standing guard.

'We know about Charlie Henderson,' Harry said as they walked in.

'Oh God, I knew they would find out,' Rose said.

'If those two had just come clean, we wouldn't be in this mess,' Amber said.

'What two?' Dunbar said. 'What are you talking about?'

The women looked unsure of themselves. 'What's happened to Charlie?' Rose said. 'Has he been... hurt?'

'Not yet,' Dunbar said. 'But he attacked an officer, so we need to know where he would have gone. I have men waiting at his place in Glasgow, but where else might he run to?'

Amber looked confused. 'Charlie wouldn't hurt a fly.'

'Maybe not, but he had a bloody good go at my officer,' Harry snapped. 'We want to know everything you know about Mhari's murder. We know she was killed in the hotel.'

Harry didn't know for sure but he wanted to see what kind of reaction that got, and he was surprised.

'We thought as much,' Rose said.

'Why didn't you speak up?' Alex asked.

'We were scared.' She looked at all the detectives. 'Somebody knows our secret.'

THIRTY-FOUR

'It was twelve years ago,' Rose said. 'At a Christmas party. One of our friends from uni had a father who was loaded and he always threw a big bash at Christmas. That year, we were invited for the weekend. It was such a good time, but Hector and Charlie had had too much to drink. And that's when it all went sideways...'

Back Then

'You know, we've watched you from afar, me and Hector,' Charlie Henderson said. 'You have to be the most beautiful young woman on campus.'

The girl laughed. 'And that's not the drink talking?'

Henderson turned to Mann. 'Tell her, Hec. She doesn't believe me.'

'You are, you're gorgeous.'

'Well, thank you for the compliment but...'

'But nothing. How about having some fun with us?'

'I'm not risking taking you to my room.' She laughed, enjoying the attention. 'I think I'd like to go back into the ballroom, if you don't mind.'

'Aw, come on, what's the rush?' Amber Dodds said. 'Have a smoke.'

The girl was unsure for a moment, but everybody else in the bedroom was smoking. So she tried it. They all laughed when she coughed.

They had music playing, not too loud to draw attention but loud enough to have their own little party. The Christmas party in the ballroom was over, but they were continuing it in the suite.

'Have another drink,' Lane Mott said, filling up the girl's glass with more champagne.

She did, and she stood up on a chair, dancing to the music. Then she overbalanced in her high heels and fell off the chair, striking her head on the edge of the vanity. She lay still on the carpet.

There was a stunned silence at first, then panic as they realised what they had done. They had given a girl booze and weed and were fully intending to have sex with her before the sun came up.

'Check her pulse,' somebody suggested, but one couldn't be found.

'What are we going to do?' Hector said. 'We're finished.'

'Don't panic.' Henderson ran a hand though his hair.

'Don't panic? Her old man's loaded. He'll have our kneecaps broken. Or worse.'

'You know who he is?'

'Yes. He's not a man we can mess with.'

'Christ. Why the fuck didn't you tell me that? What now?'

'We can't leave her here.'

'Right. Let's get her to the big fridge in the kitchen. That will slow decomposition.'

'Then what?'

'We'll dump her somewhere. Or something. We just need to hide her right now.'

The women went ahead, opening doors and keeping a lookout. The night porters hadn't got around to clearing the tables yet.

They took her downstairs and put her arms around their shoulders, as if she was drunk. Nobody came out into the corridor. They were all too busy getting drunk in the ballroom. There was a corridor that ran behind the ballroom that led to the kitchens. They took her along there. The food had been consumed ages ago, and all the kitchen staff were gone.

Charlie Henderson and Hector Mann took the young woman into the walk-in fridge, laying her down behind some shelving, way in the back, and surrounding her with boxes.

'There. If she gets found, we can say we saw her with that weird kid. That teenage freak we saw hanging about.'

'Right. Unless she isn't discovered until after we've gone.'

'We'll be gone by tomorrow morning. Then somebody else will get the blame. As long as we stick to the same story, we'll be fine.'

As they hurriedly left the walk-in fridge, the teenage boy sat further back behind the shelves. He was only looking for more wine. His mother didn't like him drinking but the odd bottle wasn't too bad. They lived on the premises and she didn't know he was sneaking out at night for booze.

He was petrified, but not half as scared as he would be if they found him with the girl. He knew he had to put her somewhere, but where?

In plain sight, that's where. Until he could move her again. Then he got to work.

THIRTY-FIVE

'She died, then you dumped her to cover yourselves,' Harry said.

Neither Rose nor Amber said another word.

'Right, we're going to have you taken to the station. We'll need a statement from you both. I'll have some of my team members formally interview you. But before you go, let me ask you something; were you all friends of Christine Farr?'

Rose looked uncertain for a moment. Then nodded. 'Yes. She was there that night. I don't know about the rest of us, but I didn't keep in touch after that night. I avoided her at uni.'

'Hector Mann certainly didn't. She was having an affair with him,' Dunbar said.

'No, she wasn't,' Amber said. 'The night she went

missing, she was supposed to meet Hector, to talk about the hotel being for sale, but that's all it was.'

'How do you know?'

'Because we were all aware that she was coming through. We were all talking about it. We were going to meet later that night, but Christine didn't turn up. Next thing we knew, she was found murdered in that park in Glasgow.'

'And you didn't think of giving us a call?' Dunbar said.

'Yeah, that's what we were going to do,' Amber said with a tone.

Harry had the two women led out by uniforms to be taken down to the interview rooms at HQ.

Ed Corbett and his wife Cat came in after the women were taken out.

'Is everything okay?' Corbett asked. 'The women seem upset.'

'We think Mhari was murdered at the hotel along the road,' Dunbar said. 'The Norwood House.'

Cat's jaw fell; any further and it would have hit the carpet. 'The Norwood? Oh my God!'

'I know it must be shocking...' Harry started to say.

'I'll say it is. My family used to own it.'

'Let's sit down at these tables,' Dunbar said and they all sat. 'Did you know what happened, back then? About twelve years ago?'

'A girl went missing. It was after a work's Christmas party. There were a lot of very drunk people. I was there that night, helping out my parents. I wasn't married at the time, and had gone back to live at the hotel with my son. That's before I met Ed and got married again.'

'Are your parents still alive?' Alex asked. 'Are they the ones selling the hotel?'

'No, they passed a few years back and left the hotel to me. I decided to sell and we bought this place. Kellerstain is more our speed now that we're getting older. Ed sold his hotel in the Highlands and we bought this together. It's a great investment; this house, the stables which we turned into the guesthouse and the two houses on the property.'

'I'm a bit confused,' Dunbar said. 'You said you invested in here, but the hotel isn't sold yet.'

'Oh, sorry. Ed bought the property with the proceeds from his hotel. I'm going to contribute when Norwood gets sold and with whatever is left over, we're going to buy property abroad. We thought we had a sale a while back, but the man who was going to buy it was killed in a car crash. It was a snowy night and his car was hit and went off the road. They found him dead the next morning. So sad.'

'You knew the group of students back then?' Evans asked.

'No, not at the time. I was so busy, and there were so many people.'

'The people you have here just now, including Mhari, you didn't know before they came to stay?' Harry said.

'No. Hector recommended them,' Cat said.

Harry looked at Ed 'We checked Hector Mann's financial records and he's living on the edge. Can I ask how he can afford to rent your house down the road?'

'He was the architect who drew up the plans for the conversion for Kellerstain to make it into a guesthouse. We got talking. He was looking to move with his wife and young family. She's a designer, so she helped put the rooms together. We came to an agreement and he rents the house for less than we would normally charge.'

'How did Charlie Henderson seem to you?' Dunbar said, wanting to throw the question in.

'Charlie was okay. Everybody seemed fine. They were friends of Hector, so they seemed legit.'

'They were at the hotel the night the girl disappeared,' Harry said.

'They were?' Cat said.

'Yes. I can't go into details, but they were there.' He took his phone out and opened the gallery to show Cat the photo of the Christmas card. 'Do you remember this?'

She looked at it. 'Yes. It was a snowman that was built next to the tree with the lights on it. We strung lights on that tree every year, but that was the first year anybody had built a snowman there. I asked my dad, why that year? and he said he didn't know. I thought it might have been my son, you know how teenage boys are, but he said he didn't know who had built it. He thought it might have been Julia's son. He was always getting into mischief, drinking and the like. But we ignored it as he was a hard worker.'

'Who's Julia?' Dunbar said.

'Julia Gregory.'

Harry looked at her. 'Julia Gregory? The woman who's a housekeeper in your house down the road?'

'Yes, that's her. Very nice woman.'

'She worked at Norwood?'

'Yes. She was the head housekeeper. She shared a little flat with her son on the property. That's why he worked for us. Only part-time mind, at the weekends and the like.'

'And she ended up working for the professor,' Alex said.

'Yes. The professor said he was looking for a house-keeper and I recommended her.'

'What happened to her son?' Harry asked.

'He's done very well for himself. Paul works for an estate agent now. Some things don't change much though; he still lives with his mother. The house down the road has an attached apartment where they live.'

'Paul Gregory's an estate agent?' Alex said. 'Do you know which firm?'

'His name isn't Paul Gregory. It's Paul Fox. His mother got remarried. He's actually in charge of selling the hotel for us. He's a nice man. He's been very diligent recently, going to the hotel to make sure everything is okay with it. No leaking pipes or anything.'

'Is he friends with Charlie Henderson?' Evans asked.

'If he is, he didn't say. And Charlie didn't mention it either. In fact, when Paul was round having dinner the other night, I introduced them to him and they all got on like a house on fire, but they didn't know each other.'

Harry stood up. 'We need to go and speak with Mrs Gregory.'

The others got up.

'Don't be offended but I'm going to have to ask you not to contact Mrs Gregory. I think she might be in danger, and you could make things worse if you call her,' Harry said.

'Oh my God,' Cat said, putting a hand on her chest. 'Is she going to be okay?'

'I hope so.'

They left the house and got back into the big patrol vehicle.

THIRTY-SIX

It might have been wise to take armed response with them, but grabbing a couple of uniforms from the crime scene outside Hector Mann's house would have to suffice. They were sent round the back with Alex and Evans.

Harry knocked on the front door and a couple of minutes later, Julia Gregory answered.

'Oh, hello, again,' she said, smiling.

'Can we step in for a moment, Mrs Gregory?' Harry said, introducing Dunbar. She let them in. 'I'll get straight to the point; where's Paul?'

'Paul? Do you need to talk to him about this awful matter?'

'Something like that.'

'Well, he was here a little while ago but then he got a call and shot off out of here.'

'What car was he driving?' Dunbar asked.

'He drives a Range Rover.'

'When you worked at Norwood, did Paul ever talk about a girl that went missing?'

'Oh, that was a terrible time. We searched everywhere for her, but no, Paul didn't talk about it.'

Harry studied her features and body language and decided that unless she was a very good actress, her son hadn't told her anything and she didn't know what he had done.

'Can you show us out the back, please?'

She walked them through the house to the kitchen and opened the door. She was shocked to see the other officers there.

'Mrs Gregory, these uniformed officers are going to take you down to the station, so you can give us a statement about what you saw or heard the night Mhari Baxter was left in front of Hector Mann's house. It's just a formality.'

'Oh, okay.'

'Do you know where Paul was going?'

'Just to his office, as far as I know.'

Harry nodded to Alex who got her phone out to call the estate agent.

They saw the Subaru parked round the side of the house. 'We'll get forensics to impound that car then they can go through it.'

'Good idea, isolating the old woman. If she finds out what he's been doing, she might have called him.'

'A mother and son bond is stronger than anything. I should know.'

'Me too,' Dunbar said. 'If I don't call my old ma every week, she makes out a missing person's report.'

Alex came up to them. 'Paul Fox is having a meeting with Hector Mann. They're going round looking at some properties that Mann has been working on, but Fox's boss can't get a hold of him.'

'Then let's go and ask Mann's wife.'

'How do you know she's home?' Alex asked.

'Because Mrs Gregory there would have the Mann kids. There's no school and she's the babysitter, according to Ed Corbett.'

'Let's go,' Dunbar said.

'I'm working from home today, but God knows, I should have sent the kids down to Mrs Gregory,' Andrea Mann said.

'We just spoke to her and she's helping us out,' Harry said as they all trooped into her house.

'What's this all about?'

They walked into the living room. Callum Mann

and his sister were sitting on dining chairs, one behind the other.

'They're playing at buses,' Andrea said. 'Better come away through to Hector's office.'

She led them back through to the hall, Alex and Evans staying with the kids.

'Use your fucking indicator, moron,' they heard Callum say, and either Andrea didn't hear or else chose to ignore it. Alice shrieked with laughter.

'Can I ask, did you and your husband move in here before he did the architectural work for the Corbetts, or did he do the work and was then offered the house at a cheap rate?'

'What are you talking about? It wasn't some business deal. Yes, Hector did the work, but he didn't get this house cheap because of it. We got it because Cat Corbett's his mum.'

'His mother?'

'Yes. They lived in the hotel. His father died when he was a young boy. Why? What's this all about?' Andrea asked.

'Hector was meeting with Paul Fox, is that right?' Dunbar said.

'Yes. Is everything alright?'

'Can you call him?'

'Yes, of course.'

'This is important; find out where he is.'

She took her phone out and dialled his number. It went to voicemail. 'Crap. He must have it switched off. He does that when he's looking round a place with a client. He gets angry when people call, so he switches it off. He'll switch it on again when he's done.'

'Do you know where he would be?' Dunbar asked.

'He only left a little while ago. He has one meeting today, at a house in Cramond. One that's just been done up. He's meeting somebody there.'

'Who's he meeting?' Harry asked, but he knew the answer.

THIRTY-SEVEN

There were two entrances to the huge property down in Barnton. One was a gravel driveway, completely covered in snow and undisturbed until Hector Mann's BMW created tracks.

The other, smaller driveway, led to the garage block, but he expected Paul Fox to drive in here, to where the front door of the property was.

The house had been rundown and had needed structural work done, which Hector had taken care of. Andrea had supervised the internal design and had done a good job. Now the owner would see a huge profit, if only Paul Fox could work his magic.

Mann got out into the cold air. Next to the house was Drylaw Park. A man walked his dog. Man and beast in perfect harmony. Maybe he'd give in and buy the kids a dog. He was wondering if they should get a chocolate Lab or maybe something smaller, like a Jack Russell, when the Range Rover pulled into the large driveway and stopped in front of the house.

Paul Fox jumped out of the car, looking frazzled.

'What's wrong with you? Sweating thinking about how much commission you're going to make?'

'Nothing. I just had a run-in with somebody, that's all. Let's get to work. I'll be fine.'

'Isn't she a beauty?' Hector Mann said as he pulled out the keys.

'She is,' Paul Fox said.

'You sure you're okay?'

'I said I'm fine, Hector. But before we go in, why don't you show me around the gardens? They're huge, aren't they?'

'They compete with anything outside the city,' Mann said. He walked round the side of the big house, leading Fox into an enclosed garden.

'There's walls on two sides, with high hedges bordering the... park,' Mann said, stopping to look at the two large snowmen that were sitting in the middle of the lawn.

They had hats on, with stick arms and carrot noses, but it was the three red buttons down their fronts that caught his eye.

'Who the hell would build bloody snowmen in the garden?' he said.

———

'It makes sense,' Harry said as Evans got his foot down. 'Hector would be able to wander about that hotel without question. Nobody would even blink an eye if they saw him in the kitchen or the bar, or wherever. He was one of the participants in that room when the girl died, he helped take her into the refrigerator, and he could have gone back and taken her somewhere to hide her.'

'Cat Corbett said they decorated the tree,' Dunbar said, 'so it wouldn't look out of place putting the snowman there, and once again, he wouldn't be questioned. Even if he was only back from uni, people would still know who he was.'

'Why would he put Mhari's corpse in his own driveway?' Alex said.

'To divert attention away from himself,' Evans said. 'If somebody did see him making a snowman, he could say it was for the kids.'

'His wife would have seen him, surely?'

'Not if she was inside with the kids,' Harry said.

'I know it all fits,' Alex continued, 'but there's some things that just don't ring true.'

'Like what?'

She sat back in the seat. 'I don't know. Something just isn't right.'

They hit the Gogar roundabout and headed down towards Barnton.

Out of habit, Hector Mann checked his phone. He'd felt it vibrate in his pocket, and normally when he was with a client, he would ignore it. But the kids had been coming down with a cold, so he wanted to check and make sure they were okay.

He took the phone out and looked at the screen before putting it away again.

'Everything alright?' Fox asked.

'Chinese tonight, or Indian. I mean, for God's sake, why can't Andrea just make a decision.'

'Women,' Fox said, laughing.

'Come on, let's get inside. I have plenty to show you. You'll see for yourself just how much quality work was put into the house. Andrea did a good job.'

He pulled out a set of keys and unlocked the front door. Inside, the heating was on, keeping the place warm.

'It's a terrific house in a terrific location. Come on, I'll show the money-maker; the kitchen.' They walked down a long hallway and into the kitchen at the back of the house.

'It looks like a lot of money was spent on it...' He stopped talking and looked at Mann.

Hector took a knife from the butcher's block.

'This is where it ends,' he said.

THIRTY-EIGHT

'What are you doing?' Paul Fox said.

Hector Mann looked at him. 'The snowmen have bodies in them. Just like Mhari Baxter was made into a snowman.'

Paul Fox didn't move. 'Put the knife down, Hector. Nobody wants to get hurt.'

'No. And if you try to grab something, I'll stab you with it.'

'Put the knife down, Hector.'

There was the sound of people coming into the large room. 'Yes, put the knife down, Hector,' Harry said.

Mann looked at Paul Fox and backed away, laying the knife down on the counter.

'Jesus, thank God you came in when you did,' Paul Fox said. 'You saw that, right? He was going to kill me.

He told me about the bodies in the snowmen out in the garden.'

'You can shut up now, Paul,' Alex said.

'Turn round,' Dunbar said.

'What?'

'You heard,' Robbie Evans said, roughly turning the estate agent round. He pulled the collar back on the man's jacket, looked at Dunbar and nodded.

Harry kept back, not wanting to go near Fox.

Dunbar pulled his cuffs out and put them on Paul Fox's wrists. 'I'm arresting you for the murder of Christine Farr, Mhari Baxter and whoever else we find out there in those snowmen.'

'What the hell are you talking about?'

'We wanted to look at your neck because whoever was fighting DS Maxwell earlier, let her get close enough to run her nails across his neck. She had his DNA under her fingernails, and now the lab has it.'

'You saw Mann with the knife! He was about to kill me.'

'I was just keeping you at bay, you mad bastard,' Hector Mann said, and Harry wondered how long it would be before his son started using that phrase. 'That was Andrea sending me a text, warning me about you.'

Fox starting wriggling until two uniforms came in and bundled him away. 'You'll all die for this!' he screamed.

'Why would you do this, Paul?' Mann shouted at him. 'We did nothing to you.'

Fox stopped struggling but the uniforms kept a tight grip on him. 'I was the boy who was hiding in that fridge when you bastards put the girl in there. I heard you saying you were going to blame me for killing her. I wasn't going to go to prison for you. They would have believed you over me because your family owned the hotel. So I took her outside in the middle of the night and built a snowman round her. Then I hid her body in the cellars and bricked it up. She's still there.'

He started struggling again and this time he was taken out.

THIRTY-NINE

The forensics team uncovered the bodies of Charlie Henderson and Lane Mott under the snow out in the back garden.

'I can't believe it,' Hector Mann said, looking out of the window where the corpses of his two friends were being uncovered. He turned back to look at Harry. 'Paul Fox was one of my oldest friends. I've known his family for years.'

'He was hiding in that fridge, trying to steal wine, when you put her in there.'

'We didn't mean anything. We were just having fun. She fell. We didn't mean to kill her. It was an accident. I know we shouldn't have got her drunk or given her weed. It was stupid.'

'You didn't kill her,' Dunbar said.

'I know, but she wouldn't have got up on the chair if she wasn't drunk...'

'She wasn't dead.'

Mann looked at him. 'What? She was. We carried her down the stairs, supporting her like she was drunk.'

'She wasn't dead,' Dunbar repeated. 'The official cause of death was hypothermia. She must have been unconscious when you put her in that walk-in freezer. Then Fox heard you saying you were going to blame him, so he made her into a snowman outside.'

'We couldn't find a pulse,' Mann said quietly. 'But we were all drunk. We probably couldn't have found our own shoelaces.'

'We're going to need statements from you and the two...' *survivors* Harry was going to say, 'women. Rose and Amber.'

Mann nodded before he was led away.

FORTY

'Here's to the happy couple,' Jimmy Dunbar said, holding his glass up. They all clinked their glasses. The Ping On Chinese restaurant in Deanhaugh Street along from Harry's place was busy but not packed.

'We're going to sit down with the team and let them know the score,' Alex said. 'Harry called Jeni Bridge, and she doesn't have a problem with us dating and working together.'

'All the best to both of you,' Robbie Evans said. 'Remember the wedding invitation. And I don't want to come along as Jimmy's guest.'

'You should be so lucky,' Dunbar said. 'I'd bring my dog along before I brought you.'

'Thanks for all your help, boys,' Harry said. 'And we got a result again.'

'Aye, you needed the Glasgow brigade to bail you

out, but that's not something you should be bragging about,' Dunbar said, grinning.

'Actually, that's not how we're going to tell it when you're back through in the west.'

'I bet you won't,' Dunbar said.

They had a laugh throughout the meal then shared a taxi along the road, dropping the two Glasgow detectives off at their hotel.

'Thanks for everything, Jimmy.'

'Nae bother, pal. I'll see you both tomorrow at the debriefing.'

'Don't do anything I wouldn't do,' Evans said.

'Christ, that opens up a world of possibilities then, doesn't it? Get in the bloody hotel.'

Harry and Alex made it into the stairwell without slipping on the ice and once inside, Harry went into the kitchen and put the kettle on. When he came back out into the living room, Alex was standing at the window looking out, with the lights out.

'I feel sorry for Vanessa,' she said. 'But I'm glad she chased you away. From a purely selfish point of view.'

'She's gone.'

Alex turned to face him. 'What?'

'She sent me a text. She's putting the house up tomorrow, but she couldn't live in it anymore. She left to go and stay with her sister in Morningside.'

'You don't feel guilty, do you?'

'A little bit, at first, but then she made the decision. I could have kept this place on and we would have gone on with our lives, but it wasn't meant to be. I felt something for her, but there was always something holding me back. I just couldn't take that next step. I can with you though. This feels completely different and I realise what it is; I wasn't in love with Vanessa. But I know I'm in love with you.'

'You don't know how much of a relief it is to hear you say that.' She closed the curtains and put the lights on. 'Now I can finally say, I'm home. For good.'

AFTERWORD

Thank you, the reader, for reading this latest Harry McNeil novel.

Piece of useless trivia – where did I get the idea for this book? I was looking at a photo or a video, I can't quite remember, but somebody had built a snowman in their front yard, and a car had driven on to the property to smash it down. The driver wasn't to know that the family had built their snowman on the trunk of a huge tree that had been cut down. And that was the spark that I needed. My twisted brain did the rest.

Many thanks to the band of outlaws I call my advance readers. You are fabulous. And thanks to my wife Debbie who once again takes care of the dogs so I can write. And to all my family who I care deeply about.

Thank you to Gail Aikman for allowing me to use

her beautiful guest house, Kellerstain Stables, in the book. Check out the guest house at www.kellerstain.com.

Once again, a huge thank you to my editor, Melanie Underwood.

If I could ask you to please leave a review that would be fantastic. As always, it helps out an author like me.

Harry will return in Hour of Need.

All the best my friends.

John Carson
New York
December 2019

ABOUT THE AUTHOR

John Carson is originally from Edinburgh, Scotland, but now lives in New York State with his wife and family. And two dogs. And four cats.

website - johncarsonauthor.com
    Facebook - JohnCarsonAuthor
    Twitter - JohnCarsonBooks
    Instagram - JohnCarsonAuthor

Printed in Great Britain
by Amazon